Brittney Lalonde was born on the island of Newfoundland in 1992 where both her parents raised her until she was 13 years of age and moved to Fort MacMurray Alberta.

Brittney loved to write ever since she was a little girl, her imagination and creativity pushed her to become the writer she is today.

When Brittney is not writing she is focused on her family life, video games and maintaining a close relationship with God.

Someday Brittney hopes to publish more novels and even some children's books. Brittney is very passionate about writing and is excited to see what she will write next.

This book is inspired by and dedicated to my amazing husband, Jonathan Lalonde. I would like to dedicate this book to him, my two beautiful kids, Marshall and Lyrica, my loving parents Kim and Vaden, my other Loving Parents Sheila and Larry, sister Christina, my brother in-law Pierre Marche, and of course, God.

Brittney Lalonde

Something About 37

Austin Macauley Publishers™
London • Cambridge • New York • Sharjah

This is a work of fiction. Names, characters, businesses, places, events, locales, and incidents are either the products of the author's imagination or used in a fictitious manner. Any resemblance to actual persons, living or dead, or actual events is purely coincidental.

Ordering Information
Quantity sales: Special discounts are available on quantity purchases by corporations, associations, and others. For details, contact the publisher at the address below.

Publisher's Cataloging-in-Publication data
Lalonde, Brittney
Something About 37

ISBN 9781645753476 (Paperback)
ISBN 9781645753469 (Hardback)
ISBN 9781645753483 (ePub e-book)

Library of Congress Control Number: 2021915214

www.austinmacauley.com/us

First Published (2021)
Austin Macauley Publishers LLC
40 Wall Street, 33rd Floor, Suite 3302
New York, NY 10005
USA

mail-usa@austinmacauley.com
+1 (646) 5125767

About the Book

This book is some fiction but based on a true story about what my husband and his family went through and how God brought them through their tough times and how he brought us both together.

Chapter 1
Avery Jonathan Langston

"You idiot!" yelled Mr. Langston at one of his many employees. "I said Monday! Not Tuesday, not Wednesday, not Thursday, not Friday! Are you brain dead?" His employee shook in terror as nearby passer goers eavesdropped outside of the office doors.

"I'm, I'm so sorry I forgot to finish the paperwork for the Tokyo investors, Mr. Langston. My mother is very sick and I have no siblings that could take care of her. My father died when I was young so I'm the only one…"

Mr. Langston cut him off in the middle of his explanation. "I don't care what's going on in your pathetic life, Foreman! The Tokyo investors are coming tomorrow and I need that report finished by the end of the day or your new job will be looking for another job, understood?"

Mr. Langston sat back in his big black leather chair and wrinkled his handsome, chiseled face in anger. Foreman quickly gathered up his papers from the table next to him and swiftly left the room.

Mr. Langston, well, Avery, was a tall, young man in his early 20s. He had dirty blonde hair which was perfectly styled and not one single hair was out of place, His bright blue eyes could make any girl melt in seconds. His voice was deep but very soft (unless he was angry). He made everyone who listened to him speak hang off every word he said. He was the definition of handsome but also the definition of a jerk. Avery came from a rich family. He was not close with his family at all, in fact, he hasn't seen his parents in over two years and they live in the same city. He honestly seemed to have it all, the looks, the money, the ladies, a huge business empire, and the nicest Lamborghini you have ever set your eyes on. But he was missing one thing, a nice personality. He was easy to anger and never thought of anyone other than himself.

Who would have thought that all would change in such a short time? Oh…you don't know? Okay, no more spoilers. Let's continue on…

Avery sat looking at the intercom on his desk fuming with anger. He rubbed his neck to try and release some of the tension he was feeling. "All right, Avery. Time to get back to business," he said aloud to himself. He smoothed out his luxury suit and pressed the little black button on the com. "Sophia, dear, could you please come into my office," he said in the sweetest voice you have ever heard.

Sophia replies with a soft, tiny voice, "Right away, sir."

"Thank you," he said as he released his finger from the button.

Sophia swooped in clicking her heels as she tried to hurry her way into his office.

"Would you like a promotion?" Mr. Langston smirked as Sophia blushed entering the room hearing those words, thinking the worse possible scenario.

"Uhm, ahhh…" she stuttered as Avery cut her off. "Get your mind out of the gutter, I need you to fire someone at the end of the business day, and a few others as well. When you do it, I'll give you a bonus on your check." Sophia looked down at her feet and shyly replied, "I, I don't know…" she was cut off a second time.

"Great!" Avery said with excitement. "Here is the list of unlucky suckers that I have no use for anymore." He leaned back in his chair and stuck out his arm, waving the paper at Sophia like he was surrendering a war. But we all know by now he's not the type to surrender to anyone easily.

"Come on, sweetheart, I don't have all day," he said in a manipulating tone.

Sophia gently took the list and turned to walk out as she quietly read the list to herself, Jimmy Harrison? Awww, he just had two baby girls last week, Scarlet Peterson? Oh, no, she is such an angel. She always brings cookies in for the staff and has those three wonderful kids she adopted… Dean Baker, Fredrick Silver, Jerry Bishop, and William Foreman? No, not William. Sophia sighed as she continued to her desk.

Sophia had long, brown hair that she always wore in a tight bun so you would never know just how long her hair actually was. She had piercing, green eyes and a natural beauty about her. She never wore any makeup (not like she needed it). Her skin was flawless. She was a pretty, petite professional. (Ha, try saying that five times fast.) She was very eye-catching but too shy to really know just how much of a catch she was.

Sophia sat at her desk fiddling with the papers and other random things. Her hands were shaking and her mind was everywhere else, except on her work. Could she fire her fellow colleagues? Sophia couldn't even tell a telemarketer to stop calling, so letting go people she worked with every day would be way too tough.

Sophia contemplated the pros and cons and couldn't think of one possible pro besides the increase in her pay check.

Sophia stood up and took a deep breath. She looked at the time on her cell phone screen and fixed her blouse. The end of the day was here and she had finally made her choice.

As she made her way down the hallway to Avery's office, William sprinted by, "Sorry, Sophia, got to get these papers to Langston."

He quickly yelled out as he kept sprinting down the hall. Sophia smiled and it quickly turned into a frown as she remembered what she had to do next.

"About time!" Mr. Langston snarked at William as he placed a perfectly organized file folder down on his desk. "Sorry, sir," William said in a quiet tone. "Whatever, leave now." Avery pointed his finger to his office door as he looked down at the folder unimpressed. William nodded and slowly walked out. As he did, Sophia was standing by the office door waiting, "Is it safe to go in?" Sophia whispered. William abruptly retorted, "Is it ever safe to go in there?" Sophia huffed in agreement, nodding her head as she took another step closer to Avery's door. She turned her head to the side as she watched William walk away in the reflection on the glass window. She let out a huge sigh and knocked two knocks on the office door with her pointer knuckle.

"What now? Didn't I tell you to buzz off, I'm busy in here," Avery shouted with anger and frustration in his voice as he forcefully opened the door knocking Sophia right off her feet. As she stumbled, she quickly grabbed the wall behind her saving herself from a total wipeout. "Oh, for heaven's sake, I'm sorry, Sophia," Avery rushed over to make sure she was all right as she fixed herself. "That's… That's fine, sir, I was just coming to talk with you for a moment."

Sophia looked down at her feet as Avery wrapped his arm around her shoulders pulling her into his side.

"You know my door is always open for you, Sophia. Please come in, sit down, and let me get you some water." Avery walked her into his office as fellow employees were leaving for the day. Avery closed the door behind him and guided her to his big office chair. "Here, sit, let me grab you a glass of water." Sophia sat in confusion while her boss walked over to his mini fridge to grab water. He then opened the cabinet beside it, grabbing two crystal glasses, and placed them on the countertop below. As he poured, Sophia quickly gazed at his suit tightening around his strong arms.

Yes, he was a jerk but damn, he was attractive. Avery walked across the office confidently and placed the two glasses of water onto his desk in front of Sophia. "Again, I'm so sorry, I didn't mean to be so aggressive I'm just really stressed out today."

He lightly took her hand in his and kissed it softly, "My apologies, beautiful."

Sophia lost in his eyes smiled and giggled "Ooh, it's okay." Blushing, she swiftly pulled her hand away from his and brought it up to her chest, cradling it with her other hand. Avery walked around his big mahogany desk and pulled a stool out from the small bar he had to the left of him and sat next to her turning his office chair so she would be facing him. "Now what brings you here," he said as he winked and smoldered placing his hand on her arm. "Ummm…." Sophia's heart started to pound as she felt his hand slowly run down her arm onto her leg. "You know, not to sound too forward, but I've wanted you on this desk for a long time." Sophia's eyes widened and her jaw dropped as she heard those words come out of his mouth. "Ex…Excuse me?" Sophia caught off guard, jumped a bit in her seat as Avery laughed at her reaction. "I noticed you looking at me, too," he lightly caressed her face and leaned in for a kiss. Sophia not able to resist his handsome face and beautiful eyes, starting kissing back. Avery quickly lifted her up onto his desk and wrapped her legs around his waist. Sophia moaned and bit her lip as one of his hands slid under her blouse. "Is this okay?" he asked for reassurance, even though his hand was already clasped onto her breast. Sophia nodded and pushed herself against his body.

After 30 minutes with the boss, Sophia quickly pulled herself together and fixed her hair. Avery sat in his office chair and stared at her in lust as she buttoned up her formed fitting blouse. "So how did they take it after you told them the news?" Avery questioned her as he fixed his tie. "Did Jerry cry?"

Sophia turned around slowly as she tucked a loose piece of her hair behind her ear. "That's what I came in here to tell you in the first place." Sophia took a few steps backwards and adjusted her skirt. "I couldn't do it, I'm sorry," Sophia looked up at Mr. Langston as he started to turn red in the face.

"You didn't do it? You know I asked you specifically to do that for me today," Avery pushed his chair back as he stood up to zip up his pants zipper. "Thanks for the fun, hun, but when you leave today, take your shit with you." Avery placed his hand lightly on her back and guided her out his office. "What?" Sophia turned to a door in her face. She felt used, dirty, and kind of sexy as she walked down the hall to her desk to pack up and leave. Now Sophia wasn't Mr. Langston's first. He has done this multiple time to multiple women, big or small, black or white, old or young, he just wanted to have fun. No remorse whatsoever.

Sophia left the building and was never seen again. Like the other girls he had been with, he only "slept" with each of them once. They were just numbers on his personal scoreboard and Sophia was number 35. Avery checked her off his list and continued on his way.

Avery grabbed his briefcase off of his desk and turned off the lights in his office. The hall was dark but the safety lights on the floor lit up just enough to see where he was going. Avery was quite exhausted since he stayed late at work finishing up his presentation for the Tokyo investors for the next morning. He leaned against the wall as he waited for the elevator. Looking at his Rolex, he yawned as the doors of the elevator opened. He slowly stepped in and the doors shut behind him. He pressed his thumb against the main floor button and slowly leaned back his head until it rested on the cold elevator steal. Avery closed his eyes until the elevator dinged and the doors slid open. He dragged his feet across the floor of the lobby as he headed out the front door. "Late night again, Mr. Langston?" one of the security guards stated as he quickly walked towards the front door. His keys jangling as he escorted him out. "Yeah, okay. Night, Barry," Avery said with irritation as he walked out to the parking lot. The guard quietly corrected him, "Its Larry, sir." Avery pulled his keys out of his pocket and waved as he opened the driver's side door and sat in his Lamborghini. This car was every man's dream. It was pure white with chrome in all the right places. It had a spoiler on the back and an option to put the top down at any moment. All the ladies loved his car and Avery loved his car more than the ladies. And that's saying something.

Avery revved up his engine and sped out of the parking lot and onto the highway. It was about a 35-minute drive from his office to his penthouse suite on the other side of town. Avery's eyes were getting heavy and so was his foot. Avery turned up the radio and put the windows down to get a fresh breeze on his face to try and stay awake. All Avery could think about was getting home to his nice, comfy, king size bed. The road was straight to his place and not many vehicles were out on the road at 1 a.m. Avery pushed the gas a little bit harder, exceeding the speed limit in hopes of making it home a bit faster than expected. Avery's tired eyes glared down at the gage, he quickly looked up to see a red light a few meters ahead. Avery wasn't fazed by this, it was late and no one was driving, he didn't care if he got a ticket, he had the money to pay for it. He just wanted to shave a few minutes of his driving time and get home. He pressed on the gas pedal even harder, his body jolting back like if he were taking off in an airplane. Avery's Lamborghini quickly brightens up as he sped through the light. A taxi cab was going through a green light at the same time as Avery and they collided. Avery instantly was knocked out by the airbag as his beautiful Lambo turned into a pile of scrap metal. It was a horrible accident. Fortunately, the taxi had no passengers but sadly, the driver did not survive the crash. Firetrucks, ambulances, police, and multiple news crews flooded the scene. Avery was still unconscious as the paramedics rushed to get him out of the car. "He's not breathing!" a female paramedic shouted over the commotion. Several paramedics ran over to Avery's aid as he lay there on the ground.

"This man needs an emergency tracheostomy. Get him on the gurney!" three medics lifted Avery onto the gurney and pushed him inside the ambulance. The ride along paramedic carefully inserted the sharp medical knife between his Adam's apple and cricoid cartilage and quickly pushed a tube in his neck as he took a breath still unconscious. "He's in critical condition now, breathing." So much going on in so little time. Sometimes, it only takes one mistake to turn people's lives upside down.

The driver of the ambulance turns the lights on and weaved down the highway passing the few cars that were on the road this late, or early depending on how you look at it. "Almost there!" called out the driver as he carefully sped through a stop sign and took a sharp turn into the hospital emergency back alley, turning off his lights as he parked near the doors. The paramedics sitting in the back pushed open the doors of the ambulance and rolled Avery out and through the emergency room doors. Doctors starting swarming around him with tools and gadgets preparing for the worse. Avery lay there, expressionless, as doctors poked and prodded him to try and save his life. "I found his wallet in his jacket pocket, his driver's license states his name is Avery J. Langston, male, age 23," a random paramedic read aloud as a nurse rushed to the information desk and quickly typed his name in. The nurse also read aloud "Blood type A+, no recent medical history, no allergies, and I'll call his emergency contact immediately." Doctors rushed Avery into another room as nurses prepared a bed for him. "If he makes it, he'll be here for a while," a concerned nurse stated as her and a few others started to put new sheets and blankets onto the bed in the Critical Condition ward.

Meanwhile, at Avery's parent's beautiful mansion, they were both sound to sleep. Suddenly Clara (Avery's mother) was awakened by vigorous vibrating from her cell phone. Clara rubbed her eyes and quickly leaned over to get the phone. "Do you know what time it is? Yes. Oh, I see… All right…"

She hung up and softly shook Weston's arm (Avery's father), "Weston, dear, wake up, Avery is in the hospital and he's in critical condition. He ran a red light." Weston rolled over and quickly sat up in the bed "I knew that boy couldn't handle a damn Lamborghini." Weston slid out of bed and quickly opened the top drawer of his wardrobe. "Let me grab some pants and will go." Clara jumped out of bed also and grabbed their keys to go. Now, before we go any further, I should give you some background information on Avery's parents. Clara grew up in a home where money was tight and things were limited, which made her grow up to be grateful for what she had and a strong but firm woman.

She was very strict as a parent as she spent a few years in the military when she was younger. She loved her son but rarely showed emotion or said, "I love you," to anyone. Her eyes were kind but her face looked stern. Her hair had a natural curl that all the ladies in the 80s would have killed for. She was brood in the shoulders but had an average frame, you could tell she was a very active woman in her younger days. Weston was quite the opposite. He was raised in a home where everything and anything was available to him whenever he wanted or needed. He went to the best schools and learned all the tricks of the trade from his father. He was very book smart and street smart, which eventually led him to Wall Street, where he made his own millions. Weston was a short man with a belly and a mustache all porn stars in the 70s had. He had short hair with handsomely grey strains all over. Clara and Weston met at a mutual friend's house when he was 20 before he got his millions and he fell in love with her grace and her hard-to-get attitude. He knew she was a strong woman and he had to have her.

They got married shortly after they met and been together ever since. You know what they say, when you know, you know. So, when Avery was growing up, his mother was very strict and his father left most of the parenting to her as he was busy with the stock market and swindling investors. Avery craved for a loving touch from his mother or a, "Good job, son," from his father but never received any of that. Maybe that's why he's like what he is today but who knows for sure.

Avery's parents quickly pull into a parking stall at the hospital and fast pace walk into the hospital's front doors.

"My son! Where's my son?" Weston shouted as his voice cracked from holding back emotion. Clara hugged into her husband and gently rubbed his back as the doctor asked for their information to make sure they were in fact whom they said they were. "Yes, your son is Avery J. Langston. Correct?" the doctor calmly replied. "Yes, where is he? Is he okay?" Weston loudly asked as his heart leaped into his throat. "Let's all go to the back and sit down for a moment," one of the nurses walked around the glass and guided them into a sitting room. Avery's parents sat as the doctor pulled out her papers and tried to explain what had happened and what is currently going on now. "We can't say for sure that he will be okay at this time, he has opened his eyes once but quickly went into convulsions and lost consciousness again. Looks like his left arm and nose may be broken due to the impact of the airbag. He has clear fluid coming from his nose and ears. He is completely unaware and unable to respond to external stimuli such as pain or light." Avery's parents both looked at each other. It was the first time in Weston's life he had seen the fear in Clara's eyes. "What, what does this mean?" Clara stuttered as she grabbed Weston's hand and squeezed. "Well, all we can really diagnose right now is that Avery is in fact in a coma. Now, he could wake up in a few hours, in a few days, or in a few weeks…" The nurse took a deep breath as the doctor continued. "Or he could possibly slip into a vegetated state or worse, depending on the damage to the brain." Clara's eyes filled up with tears as she stood up from her seat. "When can we see him?" Clara sternly asked as she wiped tears away from her face. "Right now, they are still doing a test and setting his bones back in place so they can cast it, it shouldn't be much longer now," the doctor apologized as she turned to walk away.

The nurse standing in the corner of the room followed the doctor out as Avery's parents collapsed into each other's arms.

Letting go of the emotion they had bottled up over a lifetime.

Weston eventually fell asleep on the light blue chair in the center of the room. One of the nurses brought them both blankets and pillows to use while they waited for more news. Clara couldn't sleep, she stood by the doorframe, pacing back and forth the hallway to check if the doctor was coming back. Her eyes wandered as she paced, her mind full of unwanted thoughts. Clara snapped out of it as one of the nurses gently patted her on the shoulder. "Here, have some tea," the nurse walked into the waiting room and placed a tray with two teacups, sugar packets, and creamer down on the coffee table. Clara smiled and nodded as she bent over to grab the mug and a creamer. The nurse turned to leave but stopped at the doorframe "We're all praying for your son," she kindly said as she left the room. Clara put her mug down on the table and pulled her hands up over her face as she softly began to weep. She closed her eyes and knelt down onto the floor, leaning against the table in front of her. She rested her elbows and leaned her head against her tightly closed hands. "God?" she muttered as she tried to calm herself down enough to pray. "I'm sorry for not contacting you as much as I should, you know I'm not the best at this sort of thing." She swayed slightly side to side as she continued. "We need you now, my son, he needs you now." Tears flowed as she spoke, "Please don't let him die,

I know he hasn't been closed to either one of us lately but I want to show him I can be a loving mother. I do love him. Please give us both a second chance to show love and kindness. Don't take him now, please." Clara's rested her arms and head on the table as she cried more tears. Clara knelt on the floor for an hour, repeating her prayer over and over again until she fell asleep. A few hours later, Weston opened his eyes and stretched out his arms and legs as he yawned. "Oh. Shit, I got a cramp, ugh, you would think they would have something better to sleep on in here. Shit," Weston muttered to himself as he woke up. Weston always had something to complain about, nothing seemed to be good enough in his eyes, he always thought there could be better, and they could have done better, no matter how great something was. There was no pleasing Weston, especially on days ending in "Y." Weston stood up and started to walk around the room, shaking his leg as he walked. "Frigging legs," he muttered under his breath as he shook.

Clara slowly looked up from the table and let out a little smirk as she watched her husband shake his leg like a dog with fleas. "Didn't sleep well, dear?" Clara giggled as she started to slowly push herself off the floor and onto the couch behind her. "Just fabulous!" Weston exaggerated as he limped over to sit next to Clara on the couch. Weston leaned over and kissed Clara on the forehead. "And you?" Weston looked down at Clara as she placed her head on his chest. Clara sighed, "What's sleep?"

She replied as both of them chuckled, trying to find some humor in these unsure times. As they both sat there in silence, cuddling on the couch, the nurse from the night before quietly scuffed her way into the room. "Morning," she said as she opened the blinds in the waiting room. Both, Clara and Weston, squinted as the light hit their eyes. The nurse turned and pointed to the hallway. "You both should go to the cafeteria and grab some breakfast, Its French toast day," the nurse grabbed the tray of tea she brought in the night before and placed it onto the cart that sat in the hallway. "We're soon switching shifts so the doctor that was here last night when your son was brought in will come in and brief you on what's going on and the new doctor on shift will be coming in to introduce himself to you both." Clara nodded as Weston quickly stood up to shake her hand, "Thank you, you've been very kind."

The nurse smiled and replied, "I'm just doing my job. I'll be back later tonight to check on you guys, okay? I'll keep praying."

The nurse walked out and the doctor walked in. The doctor was a young woman with olive skin and short black hair. She was average height and weight. She held her clipboard tightly in her hands as she flipped the papers back and forth reading what she had written down a few minutes before. Weston cut the silence, "So what is going on?" Clara stood up slowly as the doctor took her clipboard and placed it under her arm. "My name is Doctor Jha, nice to meet you both. So, the information we have right now is, your son is still in a coma. We did several tests and it is clear that your son has suffered very severe and very traumatic head trauma. We have done a C.T. scan and also an M.R.I. test and noticed some small bleeds in the cerebral cortex. From what we can tell, it seems your son has a diffuse axonal injury but we aren't sure." Both Avery's parents looked at each other in confusion. Before they could even ask what that was the doctor explained. “D.A.I. is one of the most devastating types of traumatic head injury. The outcome of this is usually coma with 90% of patients with severe D.A.I. never gain consciousness again. I’m sorry.”

Weston started to cry as Clara started to get angry. “No!” she yelled, “I don’t accept this. Let me speak to another doctor!” Clara barged out of the room and yelled down the hall, “Can I speak to another doctor please?” Clara kept yelling out. Weston quickly ran towards her and wrapped his arms around her to try and calm her down. “Shush, it’s okay, honey, we will find out other options and get other opinions. Shush,” Weston hugged her tight as Clara broke down in the middle of the hallway. The doctor apologized again and reassured them she would try her best to do whatever she could to help their son. The new nurse on duty tried to comfort them as she helped them both up off the floor. “Would you like to go see him now?” Sheila, the new nurse on duty softly, asked. Weston and Clara’s eyes both widened as they both nodded and followed her into another corridor. Their hearts pounded as they drew near to see their son for the first time in two years. “Here’s his room,” Sheila said as she slowly opened the door. Not knowing what to expect Avery’s parents held hands and walked in together.

“He has his own room, we set up a bed over there for you both and a chair, so you guys can be a little comfier until you decide what the plan is,” Sheila pulled back the curtain, revealing the man they raised. “I’ll leave you three alone, remember to talk to him like he’s awake, it helps some patients.” Sheila bent over and grabbed a little remote that was attached to the side of the wall,

"If you need anything, press this and I will be right there." Sheila placed the remote on the little table near the bed and left the room. Who was this man laying here? This was not the son they knew. Their son was Avery Jonathan Langston, A strong, smart, handsome businessman who always had something to say and an opinion to give. It was frightening seeing their son this way. They both took a few steps closer to Avery's bed, almost too nervous to touch him, afraid they would hurt him or break him in some way. Weston took the final step to the bed and leaned over Avery's unconscious body and held back tears as he spoke to him. "Hey, son. Its Dad," his words cracking as he talked. "We're here and were not leaving." He buried his head into his jacket and pulled the chair from the corner and dragged it next to the bed. Clara came up behind her husband and wrapped her arms around him. "We don't have to make any decisions yet." She kissed his back as they both stood there, staring at their only son.

Chapter 2
30 Days

"Good morning, Mr. and Mrs. Langston, how are you guys doing this morning?" Kimberly, the nurse, said as she brought in a bag full of liquid and swiftly switched the empty bag with the full one. "Breakfast time, Avery, you must be getting sick of the same stuff over and over again," Kim said as she went to the wall and grabbed the medium size gloves out if the box. "They are serving oatmeal today so I don't blame you for not waking up for that." Kim bounced around the room as she changed his pee bag and checked his pressure cuffs that were on his legs. "Thank you again, Kim," Clara said as she sipped on her morning tea. "Oh, no worries, this is my job. I love it." Kim grabbed some blankets from the drawer and covered Avery up before leaving the room. Clara sat drinking her tea as she flipped through the magazine, she took from the waiting room. "Hey," Weston pushed open the door with his back as he brought in the pizza he just ran and got for lunch. "I hope meat lover's is okay, it was the only one they had ready to grab and go." Weston placed the pizza down on the table and opened the box. The smell filled the tiny room and drifted out into the hallway. "It's fine, honey," Clara smiled softly as she placed her tea mug next to the pizza box. "Oh, shit, I left the drinks in the car, I'll be right back, sweetie." Weston quickly leaned down and kissed his wife as he turned to run back out into the parking lot.

Clara closed the pizza box to try and keep it warm until Weston got back with the drinks. As she did, she looked up at her son and took a deep breath. All of a sudden, Avery's blanket by his feet moved. Clara shook her head in disbelief as she looked again, standing up from her chair slowly walking closer to him. Avery's foot twitched under the blanket. Clara has seen him do this before but not as much. She quickly walked over to his side and held his hand, "Avery, it's mom. Come on now, it's time to wake up, baby." She lightly rubbed his hand as she kept talking to him, "Avery, please wake up, honey, you have had your time. Wake up!" Clara started to get frustrated. "Wake up!" she yelled across the room as her voice echoed into the hall. Weston burst through the door "Clara, what the hell are you doing, dear?" Weston threw down the bag of drinks onto the couch and made his way over to Clara by the bed. Weston grabbed her and pulled her in him and hugged her tight. "He twitched again!" Clara shouted. Weston shook his head, "He always twitches." Clara pushed herself off her husband and grabbed her son's hand once again, "Come on, Avery, wake up! We need you to get your ass up off this bed right now." Avery's eyes seemed to move under his eyelids. Both, Clara and Weston, looked at each other with shock on their faces. Weston ran to the other side of the bed and grabbed his other hand and joined in. "Avery, come on, boy, Get up! Get your shit together, boy. Don't just lay there! You're stronger than this." Both, Clara and Weston, continued to shout at Avery. Two nurses rushed in and pulled them away from Avery. "What are you two doing?" one of the nurses asked in a concerned tone.

"It's working!" Clara said as she kept screaming over the nurses. "Wake up, you lazy prick," Weston continued. The nurses shook their heads until one of them noticed Avery's eyes slowly open. "Wait, wait…." the nurse yelled, "Call the doctor in now."

The other nurse ran down the hallway as Clara, Weston, and the other on-duty nurse crowded around his bed.

Avery's eyes looked around the room but no movement or speech followed. "My boy!" Weston hugged Avery and wept. Clara stood there smiling the biggest smile she ever smiled in all of her life. "It's all going to be okay," she said quietly to herself. But little did she know, this was literally just the beginning.

The doctor entered the room. "Welcome back Avery," the doctor said with no expression on his face, looking down at his folder of papers on Avery's medical history. The doctor slips between the nurse and Weston as he takes a little flashlight out of his pocket and shines it into Avery's eyes. "Hmmmm," the doctor was staring intensely into Avery's eyes now. The doctor twitched his head towards the nurse as to say "I need them out of here." The nurse softly spoke up "Ummm… Clara, Weston, let's give the doctor a minute to check on Avery." Clara gave Avery a kiss. "We're just outside sweetie! Don't worry, dear."

They all walked out as another doctor and two more nurses entered. "What's going on?" Weston asked confused. "My boy's awake!" He smiled as he talked to the nurse almost in disbelief as he said it. "They just are doing a check. They do this for every patient in Avery's condition," the nurse sat them down on a bench in the hall. "I'll be back." The nurse slowly walked away as Avery's parents sat and wondered. Back in Avery's room, the doctors were conducting a test to see how Avery's brain was functioning. "Hello, do you know your name?" one of the nurses asked Avery as his eyes kept moving back and forth. "Hmmm… No Response."

The doctor wrote a few notes in his folder and quickly ordered a brain scan. The nurses rolled Avery's bed out and down the hallway. Clara and Weston stood up "Where are you taking him?" Clara shouted.

"Just for another scan, we will be right back," the nurse smiled and continued on her way. The nurses gently rolled Avery to his side and slid him onto the machine rolling him back onto his back. Avery didn't move much, his eyes wiggled and his toes but nothing else. "We're just doing another test, Avery. No worries, okay?" the nurse ran behind the screen and pressed the button to slide him inside.

The doctor stood back looking at the scanning computer screen evaluating the situation at hand. The nurse looked up at the doctor. "Still the same diagnosis, sir?" the doctor sighed and nodded.

"Must be a diffuse axonal brain injury, nothing really shows up on the test besides the blood spots and he seems to be still in a coma state."

The nurse shook her head in disbelief. "So, he's still technically in a coma?" The doctor nodded once again, then pointing to the brain scan on the screen, "By the damage done in this area here and also over here, it seems his memory will be affected."

The nurse pushed the button on the machine as Avery slowly starting to appear out of the machine. Avery made a few random noises as the nurses came to help place him onto his hospital bed again. "This is not going to be easy to tell his parents," the nurse said as she read the doctors notes he gave her.

Avery's parents pace the hallway as they waited for his return. "Maybe we should go grab a slice of pizza." Weston put his arm around Clara as they both slowly walked back into the room. Moments later, the doctor and the nurse roll Avery back into his spot in the room. Clara popped up from her seat like a jack-in-the-box as they entered. The doctor stepped closer to Clara, "You may want to sit back down." Clara took a step back and sunk into the couch. "What is it, doc?" Weston said looking up at him, putting his soda down onto the table in front of him. "Well…" the doctor sighed and looked down at his papers once again. "Avery seems to be suffering from Diffuse Axonal Brain injury, which we told you that 90% usually die or become vegetables, he seems to be awake but still in a comatose." Avery's parents both looked at each other, "What do you mean he's still in a coma, he is awake!" Weston shouted at the doctor in frustration. "Well, to put this in terms you will understand, it's like he's experienced Shaking Baby Syndrome as an adult. His brain was rattled in his skull during the accident and now it seems he isn't able to really function. He may be in a wheelchair and unable to do anything for himself for the rest of his life. But there is a slim chance he may be able to learn everything over again with time and therapy. So, I'm suggesting a transfer to a hospital in which they specialize in traumatic brain injury and recovery. I will make some calls and get back to you." Weston clenched his fist and headed for the door. Clara tried to grab his arm as he slipped past her and walked out, slamming the door behind him. "I understand this is very hard for both of you, honestly, you should be thankful that he is even alive in the first place. It's truly a miracle he even woke up." The doctor closed his folder, "I will try to get a medic vac here tomorrow night and one of you can fly with him. The other has to drive. It's about a five-hour drive to the T.B.I. recovery center."

The doctor walked out as Clara sunk into the couch even more. Bombarded with her own thoughts, *Will he ever walk again? Will he be able to speak or work or be independent?* Clara was thinking these things but she honestly was just happy he was alive. Clara stood up and pulled the curtain over and knelt down by the couch she was sitting on, resting her arms on the seat as she began to pray, "Lord, thank you so much for letting Avery live. Please help us through this difficult time as we try our best to help Avery return to his normal life. I know there is a slim chance but I promise I will show him all the love and support I should have given him growing up and help him recover. Please give me and Weston strength and Avery the will." Clara squeezed her hands together tightly as she prayed. Weston quietly came into the room and peered around the curtain. He stood there watching her as his eyes filled up. Clara finished her prayer and pushed herself up off the floor. Weston quickly ran over to help her. "You okay, dear?" Clara said looking up at her husband with concern. "I'm fine, I'm just worried about Avery," Weston sat on the couch putting his arm on the armrest and palming his face with his hand. "He'll walk again, He'll talk again, we got this." Clara hugged into her husband as they both looked over at Avery lying in the bed, motionless.

Clara and Weston fell asleep on the couch. Both of them snoring as they did. Avery couldn't speak so he couldn't tell them to be quiet but he was thinking it, I'm sure. His eyes focused on his parents, Avery began to try and make noise. Clara, being a soft sleeper, quickly opened her eyes. She hopped up off the couch and made her way over to Avery's bed. She sat in the chair next to him and held his hand. "We're going to do whatever we can to get you back to living a normal life, okay?" Avery twitched as she spoke.

Chapter 3
FinRose

Sheila and Kim, the nurses on duty, chit chatted back and forth as they looked through some medical papers. "Doctor wants Mr. Langston transferred over to the FinRose today," Sheila said as she flipped through more papers. "I can't believe that young man is still here, honestly, it was a miracle he survived," Kim responded as she slides the folder she was holding back into its slot. "Well…" Sheila Started, "I guess we should go talk to the parents." Kim nodded in agreement.

Back in Avery's room, Clara and Weston sat reading some books they bought at the local bookstore about T.B.Is. "According to this book, we are very lucky you're alive, Avery. I know you probably don't feel lucky right now, son, but diffuse axonal brain injuries usually don't get as far as you come. I knew you were a fighter. Always was a strong young man." Weston explained to Avery as Avery rolled his eyes. "Did you see that, Clara?" Weston smirked and nudged Clara. "Did I see what?" Clara slowly put down her book and lowered her reading glasses to the tip of her nose as she stared up at Weston.

"He rolled his eyes at me!"

Weston's smile shined as he stood up and hugged Avery. "I missed you rolling your eyes at me!" Clara looked up at her two boys and smiled as she pushed her glasses back onto her face and picked her book back up.

Knock. Knock.

Sheila the nurse popped her head around the door "Hi, how are the Langstons today?"

Clara and Weston both greeted her at the door. "Any news on what's next?" Clara asked as she took her glasses off and placed them on the top of her head. "Well, that's what we came here to talk to you about," Kim made her way around the door and gently closed it behind her. Sheila extended her arm and slowly opened her hand to guide them over to the couch to have a seat. Kim went over to Avery's bed and changed his top sheet and his pee bag. "My goodness, Avery, for someone who can't drink anything, sure can fill a bag up," Avery watched her with his eyes as she placed another pee bag onto the catheter tube. Kim pulled off her gloves and threw them in the garbage can beside the bed. Avery watched her every move. "Hey. Now, I see your eyes watching me. You big flirt." Kim laughed. As she did, Avery smirked. Everyone gasped in amazement as Avery lit up the room with his smile. "That's one amazing step closer to recovery," Sheila announced as she sat on the coffee table in front of Clara and Weston's couch.

Clara and Weston hugged into each other as they prepared for what Sheila and Kim had to say. "It's been a long 31 days here, we know, and we have seen little improvements here and there with Avery and we are so happy for him and you all," Sheila said with genuine pride on her face. "Avery has a lot of drive to get better, it seems, and we decided as a team of professionals we can no longer help Avery," Kim added as Clara and Weston looked at them confused. "So, what's the next step here?" Clara asked concerned. "Doctor Jha has already called the Fin Rose rehabilitation medical Center and booked a spot for Avery. He will be getting transferred over there tonight and will start the T.B.I. rehabilitation program. We are not sure if this will help him or not but Doctor Jha thinks it's worth a try." Clara and Weston both nodded in agreement and stood up off the couch. Kim and Shelia quickly gave them both a hug. "We are praying everything is going to be okay and we all are rooting for him here," Kim smiled as a tear fell from her eye. "See what you got me doing, Avery? You stole our hearts here." Kim sobbed as she quickly went out to the hall. Shelia gave Avery a hug and said goodbye to the Langston's. "We're off duty now so we won't get to say goodbye later. We will miss you guys and we wish you all the best." Shelia hugged Clara and Weston once more and started to walk out. Her shoes squeaking as she did so. Clara walked over to Avery with a hop in her step and hope in her heart. "Avery, we're going to work our butts off and you are going to walk, eat, and talk again before you know it. If this is the last thing I do, we're going to do it." Avery jerked his head forward, his eyes looked dazed as he muttered something out of his mouth. Clara fluffed up his pillow and kissed him on the forehead. Tonight, starts a new beginning for us and a big step to the rest of your recovery. Weston wrapped his arm around his wife and pulled her back onto the couch. "We should have a little nap, dear, I think we are going to have a busy night." Weston grabbed a nearby blanket and covered up his wife and himself with it. They snuggled up under the thin brown blanket and quickly fell asleep. These 31 days were exhausting and it was about to get even more tiring.

Avery looked around the cold, hospital room's white walls. His eyes slowly moved to look at the tiny television above him that was on the cartoon channel. His eyes wandered to the left to look at his parents on the couch fast asleep. He sighed. He couldn't even think of any words to say, let alone say them. He was frustrated, confused, and uncomfortable.

The T.V. flashed in the under lit room as sounds or babbling came from Avery's mouth. I'm not sure what he was saying but I'm sure it wasn't good. Avery wiggled his body a little and strained his eyes to the little button on the table near his bed. He grunted as his arms moved up and down. As he waved his arms, he mistakenly knocked the remote onto the floor. Clara jumped up off the couch, tangled up in the blanket, she fell to the floor. "Oof!" Clara tumbled onto the floor. She twisted her body to face the ceiling and just laid there for a minute. Clara sighed as she closed her eyes and ran her hand through her hair. Weston yawned and opened his eyes looking down at Clara on the floor. "Honey, stop hogging the blankets and get up off the floor." Weston shook his head as he stretched his arm out to help her up. Clara quickly grabbed his hand and pulled herself up. Avery laughed at his parents. Both, Clara and Weston, laughed as they walked over to Avery's bed. "I bet you would love a steak right now, wouldn't ya, boy?" Weston taunted as his own stomach grumbled. Avery looked around the room, lifting his arms up and down as he did. "Good job, baby," Clara smiled and helped Avery lift his arms above his head. Clara got lost in thought.

Just as she switched arms, two nurses came into the room. "The medic vac will be here shortly, we need to roll Avery out to the elevator and bring him upstairs to get him ready for the flight," the nurse smiled at her and her co-worker pulled the curtain all the way over and unlocked Avery's bed wheels. "I better get my shoes on then and run back to the house and grab some more clothes before I drive out." Weston stood up and slid on his shoes as he yawned. "Could you please go to Avery's house and grab him some comfy clothes as well?" Clara asked as she gave Weston a kiss before heading out the door following the bed down the hall and into the elevator.

"Drive safe!" Clara yelled out across the hall as she walked at the nurse's pace. Weston nodded his head and waved as he walked the opposite way. Avery, Clara, and the two nurses headed into the elevator and rode all the way to the top of the hospital. As they got closer to the exit door, Clara's heart raced. Reminders of the military played in her head as she heard the sound of the helicopter's roader's spin. That was a scary time in her past but Avery's accident still scared her the most. A man waiting at the end of the hall pushed open the two wide doors and held them, so it would be easier for the ladies to push Avery's bed through. The wind gushed across their faces, blowing their hair in front of their faces. "Whoa!" one of the nurses said as she shouted, trying to be heard over the noise. "Okay, Clara. This is Pierre and this is Chris, they will be getting you both to the FinRose." Clara shook their hands as the other nurse pointed to the taller man with the scruff wearing a blue medic shirt. “This is Chris, he will be sitting in the back with you guys for the flight.” Clara nodded as Chris grabbed Avery’s bed and started to push it towards the copter. Next, she pointed to Pierre. He was a blocky but handsome man with dark brown hair and a beard to match. His eyes shined in the moonlight as he smiled at Clara. “Pierre will be your pilet, flying you tonight, he’s haven’t had an accident yet so you guys should be fine.” Pierre chimed in “Well, nothing yet anyways,” he smirked and nudged Clara like she was in on the joke. But Clara was indeed not and a little skeptical. The nurses waved and headed back inside as Pierre guided Clara into the medic vac and helped buckle her up. He closed the side door and pulled a huge lever to lock it. Chris locked Avery’s bed wheels and clipped his bed bars onto restrains and gently restrained Avery so he wouldn’t fall out of the bed. “All good to go, Pierre buddy,” Chris said through his headphone mic. “10-4. Roger that,” Pierre replied as he pushed a bunch of buttons and pulled a big black lever upwards, they lifted off. “Should only be about 20 minutes, give or take,” Pierre spoke through the intercom. Clara Leaned over in her seat as far as she could and stretched to hold Avery’s hand. Avery sighed and closed his eyes. “Get some rest, Avery, tomorrow, we start your rehab, you’re going to be back to yourself in no time.” She rubbed his hand and gently let it go as she sat back in her seat and rested her head onto the seat headrest. Chris watched Avery’s vitals all the way to FinRose Hospital’s helipad. Clara and Avery slept all the way there.

“Okay, Avery, Clara, we are here,” Chris said as he opened the door to exit the Copter. Pierre lowered the ramp as Chris released the straps from the steel bars and started rolling Avery down the ramp and into the building. Pierre quickly ran up the ramp and helped Clara unbuckle her safety belt. "Here you go, darling," Clara smiled and thanked Pierre as he held her arm and guided her down the ramp slowly. Clara quickly walked to the door that was on top of the hospital's roof. Chris was waiting behind the door with Avery. He continued to roll Avery down the hall and stopped at a reception counter. There were three computers lined up in a row and three empty uncomfortable looking chairs beside each one. The hall lights were bright and the air was humid. As you walked, the air stuffed your nose. "Check in, Avery Langston!" Chris yelled out, leaning over the counter. A short, young nurse popped out from the back room, holding her sports bottle filled with something other than water. Her hair in a thick, curly ponytail swayed back and forth as she quickly made her way to the computer in front of Chris.

"Sorry, hun, we are all on break here. Didn't hear you guys come in," the young nurse placed her bottle on the desk as she sat on one of the chairs. She twirled around in the chair and pulled herself into the desk and placed her newly manicured hand on the mouse. "Oooo, those nails look funky, Christina," Chris joked as he leaned over even more on desk somewhat flirting with her. Christina glanced down at her nails and wiggled her fingers, looking at them in awe. "Yeah, I wanted to try something different this time." Christina then quickly stood up off her chair and reached her hand over the desk counter. "I'm so sorry, how rude, I'm Christina, the floor mother or head nurse on duty tonight. We've heard so much about you guys and we are excited to help Avery get back on his feet," Clara smiled, took a step forward, and shook her hand. "Thanks, we are excited, too," Christina smiled back and quickly flopped back onto the chair. She turned back on from them as she shouted "Maddison? Joel? Can I get one of you to make sure 203 is clean and ready for Mr. Langston and his family please?" Another young nurse with beautiful long blonde hair and dimples in her cheeks came out of the back room. "Sure thing," Maddison skipped down the hall with her clipboard in hand. Christina started typing into the computer. The keys sounded angry and she pressed hard onto them as she wrote. "Ease up, killer," Chris joked again, looking down at her. "Don't you have a job to do?" Christina quickly responded, looking up over the desk as she typed. "I'll take the hint," Chris smiled and pushed himself off the desk and winked at Christina. Christina shook her head. "Nice meeting you, Clara and Avery. I wish you guys all the best on your journey." Clara nodded and softly smiled. "Thank you, Chris, Stay safe."

"You betcha!" he winked and smiled at Clara as he turned to walk away.

"So, he's all checked in now. Just give Maddie a few minutes to get the room in tip-top shape for you guys,"

Christina took a sip from her bottle and grabbed a few papers from the printer. Clara yawned as she watched. After 15 minutes of standing, waiting for the check-in to be completed, Madison skipped back down the hall towards them. "All done, Christina," Madison looked at Clara and leaned in to whisper in her ear. "I heard you guys weren't too comfy sleeping on that little couch at the other place so we made sure you guys have a room to yourselves and we put a pullout couch in there with lots of blankets and pillows, so you guys can sleep a little better here," Clara smiled as her words hit her ears.

"Thank you so much!"

"No worries," Madison scuffed her way back to the back room. As she went in, Joel, the other nurse on duty, walked out. His hair was a little shaggy, kind of covering one of his eyes. He was very tall and looked like he should be playing basketball instead. Joel walked around the corner and grabbed Avery's bed. "Ready to go, guys?" Clara nodded in agreement as Joel started to push Avery to the other end of the hall. "I'll come in to check up on you both shortly," Christina loudly stated, waving at them as they walked away. Clara waved back and so did Avery. Clara's heart filled with joy as she watched her son wave his arm like a flag. Nurse Joel stopped in front of a door and push a little green button beside it. The door opened to reveal a beautiful room filled with color and light. "Wow!" Clara exclaimed, "This room is beautiful!" Joel Smiled as he pushed Avery into the room. He started hooking up all his equipment. "Yeah, it's the nicest room we have here." Joel locked Avery's wheels and turned towards Clara. He went quiet as he spoke. "So, at the other hospital, the doctors were telling us that your son had to have eight bags of food a day and he is losing significant weight. We don't want that here. We need him eating real food so he can put some weight back on."

"So, what are you saying?" Clara asked. Joel stepped back and smiled at her as he thought of what to say next.

"We're, ahh, we are going to take out his tube tomorrow afternoon and start feeding him normally. It's really the first step to his recovery so he can gain the weight back and become stronger."

Clara looked over at Avery, then looked back at Joel. She was speechless. She had nothing to ask or say about it. Joel patted her lightly on the back, "I'm going to leave you guys alone for a bit to get some rest. The lever for the couch is on the right-hand side, all you have to do it pull it upward and the bed will pop out. Just fold it down after it pops and the mattress will inflate. Blankets, pillows, and towels are in the closet to the left and if you need anything at all, you can press the button right above Avery's bed." Joel leaned over Avery and pointed to the button.

"Thank you, again," Clara said as her voice cracked. Joel walked out of the room and gently closed the door. Clara walked over to Avery and gave him a kiss. "Get some rest, sweetie, your father should be here in a bit."

Avery nodded over and over as she spoke, closing his eyes as he did so. Clara walked over to the bathroom and lightly closed the door behind her. She made her way over to the shower and sat on the seat that was attached to the wall. She grabbed her phone out of her pocket and started to dial Weston.

Brrrrringggg. Brrrriiinngggggg

"Hey, where are you now?" Weston's voice breaking with bad reception responded. "I'm jus…ulled…over about three hours…way."

Clara intensely listened as he spoke broken words. "You have pulled over about three hours away?" Weston sounded tired and dragged out as he replied. "Think…might…have a nap…here." Clara agreed, "Yes, have a nap there, dear, don't drive tired. As long as you get here safe." Weston's phone cut out as Clara waited for his response. “Oh, shoot!” Clara muttered as the phone screen turned black. She sighed and made her way to the couch. As she pulled the lever of the couch bed, her phone vibrated in her pocket making her jump. She unfolded the bed and went to the closet to grab some blankets and pillows. After she laid them on the bed and fixed the sheets, she pulled out her cell and looked at the main screen. It was a text from Weston. It read *“I love you.”* Clara blushed and slowly texted back *“I love you, too.”* Weston and Clara hated texting. It was a “young” person game and they only did it when it was absolutely necessary. Clara’s eyes were so heavy now as she placed the phone on the table beside her. She sat on the bed, looking over at Avery one more time before she flicked the switch to turn the lights off. It didn’t take long for her to pass out since she was utterly exhausted. A few moments of sleep later, the nurse, Christina, peeked her head around the door. “I’ll let them sleep,” she whispered to herself and quietly closed the door.

Chapter 4
Road to Recovery

Around five a.m. Weston quietly scuffed into the rehab center and made his way up to the front counter on the main floor.

"Excuse me, sir," Weston interrupted as two males who looked like doctors stood chatting by the desk.

They both turned. "My name is Doctor Chang; how can I help you?"

Chang was a handsome, young doctor about 30 years of age and 5 ft., 11 inches tall. He was a strong Asian man who seemed to have grown up in this country. He spoke with a soft but firm voice. Weston was secretly envious of the young man's physique but continued, "I'm looking for my wife and son, they arrived here about one to two a.m. Avery Langston and Clara. I believe she said she was on the second floor." Weston pulled his arms out of his jacket and stuffed it under one of his arms, carrying it like a jacket baby.

Doctor Chang jerked his head and rubbed his neck as he searched the info on the computer.

"Ahhh, yes, Room 203, I have to run up there now anyways and prep a set for one of our patients, so I'll show you where."

Weston nodded and thanked him as they both walked around the desk towards the elevator in the back of the hall.

"I'll talk to you later, Mr.Pinksen," Chang lifted his palm up as if to wave but didn't. Weston and Chang both stepped into the elevator as the doors slide shut behind them. "I'm sorry to hear about your son, we will try our best to help him here." Chang placed his hand on Weston's back. He lightly slides it off as the doors of the elevator opened and walked out pointing to the door to the left. "Right in there, Weston… See you around." Weston nodded and slowly made his way up to the door. Trying not to wake anyone, Weston slowly squeezed through a little crack in the door, guiding himself with the light on his phone. Weston tip toed across the room and laid down his jacket and bags he was carrying next to the pullout couch. Weston shuffled his way between the couch and Avery's bed, trying to make his way over so he could lay down with Clara. Weston leaned over the bed and kissed Clara. As he did so, Clara jolted upward, head-butting Weston right in the face. Clara screamed!

"Settle down, Clara, it's just *me*!" Weston shouted as he fell back onto the bed, holding his face in his hands. Clara quickly stood up and flicked the switch to the lamp next to her would lighten up the room so she could see if this man was actually Weston and not some creepy nurse looking for a free kiss.

"I'm so sorry, Weston, you scared me," Clara held her chest as her heart pounded.

"I'm sorry to, hun, but shit, who did you expect? Obviously wasn't me."

Weston kind of chuckled as he grunted in pain. Clara quietly laughed as Weston wiped the blood from his nose onto his sleeve. "I think we should take you to the E.R." Weston sat up and nodded. "I think I have seen the hospital down the street from here we can walk." Weston pushed himself off the bed and walked into the bathroom to grab some toilet paper to stuff up his nose. Clara and Weston walked down the hall and stopped at the desk. Christina, the nurse, was still on duty.

"Would you be a dear and keep an eye on Avery, we have to go to the hospital, we had a bit of an accident."

Clara smiled at Weston as he muttered under his breath. "Sure thing!" Christina replied as she continued working on whatever she was working on. Weston and Clara both walked back down the hall and into the elevator, making their way to the E.R. down the street. "Seems like we have been living in the hospitals lately, huh?" Weston muttered.

"Technically, we have been," Clara responded as she sighed. A few hours later, Weston and Clara returned to the rehab center. "I can't believe you broke my nose," Weston said in amazement over and over again. Clara smiled and shook her head. "Now you know, for sure, I am a force to be reckoned with."

Weston touched the funny looking cast on his nose and replied. "I knew that from the start, that's one of the reasons why I married you." Weston blushed as Clara kissed him carefully, making sure she wouldn't bounce her nose off of his. As they headed out of the elevator and into the hall on their way back to the room, one of the nurses jogged towards them. "Oh, you're back, great!" the blonde nurse with bright blue eyes said, seeming almost out of breath. "We wanted to remind you we are taking Avery's feeding tube out today and hopefully, start him on some somewhat solid food." Clara nodded, she remembered. "Well, they are planning on taking it out now, we just wanted to confirm this with you before actually going ahead." Clara nodded once again as the nurse smiled "Great. I'm Becca, by the way, and I will be one of Avery's personal nurses. I will be working morning shift with him most of his time here." Becca shook their hands and turned and headed back towards Avery's room. Clara and Weston followed closely behind. Nurse Becca pushed open the door, she squeezed her way through doctors and nurses surrounded Avery's bed and room. "Why so many?" Weston questioned.

Becca turned and replied, "It's just precautions. Also, we are just planning our schedules to make sure the right people are helping Avery, so he can recover quickly in the best and most effective way possible."

One of the doctors held Avery's hand as he spoke, "This will be quick okay, bud, it may feel uncomfortable for a sec." He then pulled the tube out of Avery's throat as he urged, "Sorry, bud, Sorry."

Avery shook his head and urged again as the tube was fully pulled out. Clara raced over with the trash can from the bathroom. "Throw up in this if you need to, honey," Clara brought the can up closer to his face. Avery pushed it away and shook his head. Clara nodded, "Okay, okay, honey." Clara placed the can onto the floor next to the bed as the nurses and doctors dispersed. Becca went over to Avery and rubbed his back, "It's okay, sugar, we're going to get you eating real food today." Becca hugged Avery as he smiled. "He can totally understand me," Becca added. Clara and Weston acknowledged her comment. "Sure, seems that way," Weston replied.

Clara walked over to his bed and flopped down aside of him. "What can we try to feed him?"

"Well, we are planning on trying applesauce today and go from there." Becca walked over to the wall and grabbed some gloves out of the wall. She pulled them on and walked back over to Avery. "Open your mouth, sweetie, I have to check to make sure there are no sores or rips when taking out the tube." Becca lightly pulled open his jaw and used her pointer and thumb to separate, spreading apart his cheeks to have a look, "Hamm. Looks good to me, cutie." Becca winked at Avery as she pulled off her gloves and threw them in the trash. "All good here." Becca looked at Clara lying next to Avery. "I'm going to go talk to Doctor Nagy and see what she has to say, then we can get him something to eat."

Becca left the room in a hurry and closed the door hard behind her. Clara sat up in the bed cuddling into her son. "You have to try and eat, okay?" Clara looked up at Avery as he looked down at her. He shook his head *no*. "Excuse me?" Clara sat up even straighter, looking straight into his eyes. Avery kept shaking his head. "I know you just didn't shake your head at me." Avery let out a huge laugh as his mother lectured him like old times. "When your mother tells you to do something you do it, mister!" Avery let out a chuckled again as she kept telling him off. "You will eat whatever they give you so you can go home and live a normal life, *got it*?" Avery nodded *yes* and laughed once again. Clara laughed, enjoying his responses just being here at the rehab center brought hope to Clara and also Avery.

A few moments later, Becca came back into the room with a tray full of random foods.

"Here's your lunch, King Avery. We have a smoothie, apple sauce, chicken broth, and some lime Jell-O."

Heather smiled at Clara as she placed the tray down on the table beside Avery's bed. Becca sat on the bed next to Avery, pushing his hair out of his face, "Looks like you are going to need a haircut soon."

Avery jerked in the bed and his eyes glisten. He set himself up in the bed and looked over at Nurse Becca. Her blonde hair and blue eyes really stood out to Avery, not to mention her large chest pushing out on her uniform.

Becca opened the applesauce and scooped a little out with a spoon. Clara watched anxiously as she did so. "Open up, buttercup," she smirked as Avery shook his head. He just wanted a steak, not baby food. Becca tried once more. "Come on, King Avery, one bite?" she leaned in a little closer, hoping he would open his mouth. "Come on, sweetie. You can do this. It's not hard." Avery moved his hands, placing it over his quick springing erection. "Oh my!" she giggled. "At least we know that still works fine." She giggled again as she stood up to place the applesauce back on the tray. Clara shook her head in shame, "I'm so sorry, Becca."

"No, no, it's fine! I'm happy to have helped!" Becca smiled again, grabbing the smoothie and a straw up off the tray. "How about this?" she leaned in and placed the straw by his mouth, Avery didn't budge. After 30 minutes on trying, Clara and Becca were both getting frustrated. "Come on Avery, please eat for me," Heather whined as Avery shook his head once again. "I'm going to go and give him a break, and I'll try again in another 30-40 minutes." Becca pushed the tray over to the end of the table as she stood up to leave. "I'll be back for you, Avery."

Heather winked as she spoke. Avery's eyes brows wiggled in excitement as Becca and Heather left the room. He was loving this kind of attention. He hadn't had it for a while now.

"Listen here!" Clara shouted at Avery as he was lost in thought. "I'm going to look for something I know you like and will eat, get ready because when I get back you *will* eat!" Clara marched out of the room with a determined look on her face, she was tired of this and needed Avery to get better now. Weston came in through the door as Clara left. "Whoa, you on a mission, babe?" Clara nodded and continued on her way. Weston smiled as he shook his head. He came into the room and plopped on the couch. "Hey, bud, you eat yet?" Avery shook his head. "No? Why not?" Avery stared at his father but said nothing. Clara burst through the door with three different pudding cups. Weston shook his head once again and leaned back in the couch. "Here we go, buddy," Weston smirked and closed his eyes.

"Okay, I have vanilla, chocolate, and butterscotch. Pick one or I'll pick for you!" Avery looked at his mother with wide eyes. Pudding cups? He hadn't had one of those in a while either. Pudding and ice-cream were his guilty pleasures. Avery lifted up his hand and grabbed the butterscotch from his mother. "Good," Clara said as she laid down the other cups of pudding onto the tray. Clara quickly ripped the top off and scooped a spoonful into the plastic soup. "Open your mouth." Avery stared at the pudding cup. "Open now!" Clara was not in the mood for this game he seemed to be playing. Avery quickly opened his mouth. As he did, Clara shoved the pudding into his mouth. "Now swallow!" Avery's face squished together as he tried to remember how to swallow the pudding. In just a few moments, Avery was motioning for another spoonful. Clara felt accomplished and Avery did also. Becca slowly walked into the room with a bottle of water and a straw. "What a good boy! I'm so proud you finally ate something!" Becca rushed over to Avery, giving him a hug! Avery liked her hugs. "This is a huge step forward for you!" Clara's eyes filled with tears as she fed him another pudding cup. Weston would have been super thrilled about this I'm sure, but he was sound asleep on the couch. Avery was also super thrilled to see Becca again. He didn't say anything but he sure showed it.

"Avery, behave!" Clara shouted as Avery had another one of his erections. Clara shook her head, hiding her face in her hand. Becca sat on the other side of Avery, holding the bottle of water with the straw up to Avery's face. "Here has a sip," she softly suggested as she leaned in, brushing her breast against Avery's chest. This was not helping the situation at hand, but no complaints from Avery.

Within a week, Avery was eating soft solids. Mashed potatoes, cut up hot dog wieners, and even pancakes. He was even speaking simple answers. "More syrup, Avery?" Christina, the nurse, asked as she held the container of syrup over his plate. "Yes," Avery said smiling. He was even cutting up his own food. Recovery was going faster than anyone ever expected. Avery was motivated to get back to his normal life, just as much as everyone else was. Christina poured the syrup as she spoke, "So you start rehab tomorrow with Reskims. He is the best rehabilitation doctor in this country, He might seem a little stern but he is a really nice guy."

Christina flipped the top back on the syrup as Avery ate his pancakes. Weston was cleaning up the bathroom of his hair after his shave. He popped his head around the doorway, "Tomorrow? That's great pal." Avery nodded, "Yeah."

Avery looked down at his pancakes and swirled around the syrup in his plate with his fork. "You are going to do great, Avery," Christina patted him on the back as she spoke. "I promise it will be a lot better than laying in this bed." Christina grabbed the empty plate from Avery as he ate his last bite. She quickly placed it on the tray and walked it out to the cart, waiting in the hallway, "I'm going to check on my other patients I will be back soon." Avery leaned back in his bed fidgeting with his fingers as he did so.

Weston turned off the light in the bathroom and made his way to the chair next to Avery. Weston gently pulled Avery's hands apart and set them down on the side of the bed, "Relax, son, it's going to be great." Weston sat back in the chair as Avery's eyes wandered around the room.

"Mom?" Avery asked in a concerned tone. "Oh, don't worry, she will be back, she just had to run out and grab some supplies. You know, toothpaste, some snacks, body wash, and some entertainment. Like a coloring book or cards." Avery nodded and looked down at his feet, He wiggled them under the blankets. "No Good," Avery sighed and looked up at his father. "Don't think like that, son, you will. It may take a few tries but you are going to do it, I'm sure." Weston stood up and grabbed a book off the table across the room, he scuffed his way back to the chair, and flopped back into his seat. Avery took a deep breath and closed his eyes. Shortly after closing his eye, Avery was wakened by the sound of a friendly nurse, "Hey, sweetie, time for lunch," Becca placed the tray down in front of him and placed a spoon in his hands. "Here's some chicken vegetable soup. Honestly, for hospital food, it's really good." Avery smiled. Boy, was he glad to see Becca again? She was as perky and beautiful as usual. Becca placed some crackers next to his bowl and gently placed her hand on his back. "Here's some crackers if you're feeling adventurous." Avery started to feel flushed as she slides her hand off of his back. Weston shook his head at Avery as Becca grabbed some gloves from the wall. She slid them on her hands and quickly lifted up his sheet to check his catheter, "Bag is full, time for a change." She swiftly and gracefully pulled the bag out from under the blanket and switched it with a new one. "Tomorrow is the big day." Avery looked confused as she kept talking. "Going to try and learn how to walk and use the bathroom again!" Avery felt shame as he listened to her talk. He pulled the blankets up over his face to hide. Weston laughed, "Forgot you had to actually get up and go pee?" Avery shook his head under the blankets. "It's okay, son," Weston leaned forward and rubbed his leg gently. "It's all good, boy," Becca smiled at Weston as Avery hid. "Tomorrow morning, someone will come in and take the catheter out. We will just use adult diapers starting tomorrow until you can use the washroom on your own. Or at least let us know when you need to go." Weston nodded.

"See, son, all good."

Avery flopped back onto the bed. "No," Avery muttered under the blankets. Weston pulled the blanket off of Avery's face, "You gotta do what you gotta do, boy." Avery scratched the top of his forehead, "Yeah." Becca left the room as they spoke to one another. Avery was nervous about tomorrow but was excited to start living again. Avery rested his arm over his eyes as he laid back and closed his eyes once more. "Get some rest, son. You will need all your strength for tomorrow." Weston leaned back and continued reading as Avery slowly drifted off to sleep again. Avery woke up long enough to welcome back his mother from the store and to eat his supper but fell back to sleep quickly afterward.

Chapter 5
Stronger

The next morning, Avery woke up to the sun beaming into the room and a slight heat on his face. He opened his eyes and let out a yawn. He stretched his arms above his head and pulled himself up with the bar above him. Avery looked around the room. Clara and Weston were still asleep on the couch. Avery finally had a moment to himself, what would he do with his "alone" time. Avery reached over to grab the television remote and turned on the T.V. He flicked through the channels until the news popped up. Avery stared at the television as the hot news lady spoke about the weather.

"Temperature today is currently 20 degrees Celsius. With a high of 25 and a low of 14. Speaking of low, Langston stock is lower than ever with a fall out of over 82%. Other stocks like Vaden tech and Pollard Holdings and rising with a 45% increase."

Avery tilted his head at the screen "Langston." He thought to himself as he continued to watch the newscast. The lady on the screen was very entertaining to him. She was a little chubby with bright, green eyes and legs for days. Her hair was brownish red with a slight wave throughout. Her lips looked soft as she reported the news. Avery felt a tingle in his spine and a strong urge to touch his cock. Avery slid his hands down his stomach and slowly reached for his hard member. He started rubbing it as he watched the lady on the screen. He wrapped his manly hands around his bulging cock and started stroking it up and down getting slightly faster with each stroke.

"In other news, it's been over a month since Avery Langston's deadly car crash. He still is in the hospital and sources say he will never work again and will not be returning to his company. Multiple contract companies are suing for promised business income and loss work due to this horrible accident. The Langston Company is in big trouble and looks by the end of these lawsuits, Mr. Langston will have lost it all. Millions of dollars gone."

Avery quickly let go of his member as he heard his name on the television. He held his head in his hands as a sharp pain cut across his head like a knife.

Avery yelled as a flash from his past quickly appeared in his head. Avery's eyes started to tear up as he remembered his work life.

He picked up the remote off of the bed and switched the T.V. off. He didn't want to hear any more. And he definitely wasn't in the mood to…you know.

Clara and Weston jolted up out of bed when they heard Avery yell. "Avery calm down, it's okay," Weston grabbed Avery's hand to comfort him. Avery started to take deep breaths as his father rubbed his hand with his thumb. Clara gave Avery a kiss and moped her way to the bathroom. Avery looked at his father with fear in his eyes. "Who?" Avery asked, his father smiled as he spoke softly, "Who what?"

Avery replied, "Me!"

Weston Spoke, "Doesn't matter who you were. Only today matters and whom you become." Avery sighed and looked down at his hand. Weston lifted Avery chin up, "No worries, it's all taken care of." Avery leaned back down in his bed as Christina, the nurse, popped back into the room. "Morning!" Christina the nurse brought in a tray filled with food. "Today, we are serving eggs, hash browns, and bacon. We cut the bacon up for you just in case." Christina placed the tray down and left the room. Avery looked at his plate, he wasn't in the mood to eat. He was excited to go back to his normal life but the news made it seem like a scary place to go back to. The flash he had of his business and he can't even remember how he created it in the first place. Things were getting confusing for Avery and a little overwhelming. Avery started to tense up as he stared down at his plate of food. Clara and Weston watched from the corner of their eyes as Avery morph from a calm, positive boy to a very intense stressful man. "Hey, Avery what's on your mind?" Clara rushed over and started rubbing his back softly, trying to calm him down. Avery pushed the plate to the side, "Me."

He turned to his mother. His eyes widened and fear struck his face. "Who?" Avery started to cry as his mother pulled him in for a tight embrace. "Oh, honey, everything will come together soon for you, okay? You are going to have some confusing days as time goes on but soon, you will be back to your usual self." Clara pulled him tighter as he wept in her arms. Weston stood up and watched his wife and son embracing each other from a distance. Weston acted like he wasn't concerned but deep down, he was. Weston always tried to stay strong for his wife since she had to be strong most of her young life in the military. He may seem like a tough cookie to crack sometimes, but deep down, he was a pile of mush.

Christina and Nurse Joel knocked on the door as they rolled in a wheelchair into the room. Clara kept hugging into Avery until he gently pushed her off of him. Christina pointed to the curtain. Soon after she did, Joel quickly yanked the curtain over to give Avery some privacy. Christina rolled the wheelchair closer to Avery's bed just outside the curtain. "We are going to take the catheter out now and slide on another one of these babies," Christina pointed to the disposable diapers. Clara nodded and Weston sat down as the nurses prepared Avery to stand up for the first time in over a month. "This may hurt a little," Christina said as she gently removed the catheter. Avery groaned as they removed it and placed another diaper on him. "Okay, bud, time to stand up and get dressed." Joel bent over to grab Avery's arm. He quickly wrapped it around his neck and gently pulled Avery upwards, sitting him on his butt. Christina held Avery's back as Joel pulled Avery's legs and slide them off the side of the hospital bed. "You all right, hun?" Christina asked in a sweet, concerned tone. "Yeah," Avery nodded as he tried his best to help them. Joel wrapped both of his arms around Avery like he was going to give him a bear hug. Christina quickly ran around to the other side of the bed and pushed the wheelchair closer as Joel tuned Avery's back towards the chair. "All right, my dude. Almost there," Joel gently placed Avery on the chair and smiled. "Let's get your socks, pants, and shoes on first, then we can work on the easy stuff." Avery agreed. Clara popped up and speed to the table and pulled out the drawer with Avery clothes inside. She yanked out some socks and picked out an outfit for her son to wear. "Here, I'll put on his clothes and you hold him up for me," Clara ordered Joel. Joel happily did as he was told. Avery watched as his mother pulled his socks up over his feet. She put his pants on one foot at a time and pulled them up to his knees. Joel lifted him up and Clara swiftly pulled them up the rest of the way. Joel placed him back down as Clara grabbed the shirt and yanked it over Avery's head. "Good?" Clara asked. Avery nodded once more as he was finally dressed. And ready to rock. Well…walk.

"Okay, we will let Dr. Simms know you are ready to start and we will come back and get you in ten."

The door makes a loud thud as it closes behind them. Clara walks over to Avery as he sits examining his chair. "Try pushing the wheels," Clara suggests.

"I don't know," Avery replied, looking down at his hands. Weston walks over with excitement in his face.

"Let me show you how it's done." Weston quickly exits the room and returns moments later with his own chair. Clara shakes her head, "How about if someone else needs that chair, Weston?"

"They have a tone of 'em here, they won't miss this one," Weston reassures her as he zooms past in the chair. Avery watches his father play like a child in the chair, studying every move he makes. Clara moves the couch over to give them some more space.

"Come on, son, try it!" Weston rolled past him once more. It looked like fun and Avery wanted to try. He placed his hands on the wheels and pushed with all his might. He may have been down for the count for a while but he was still as strong as ever. Avery leaned forward a little as he wheeled his way across the room. "That's it, son!" Avery may have forgotten how to do a lot of things but having fun wasn't one of them. Avery kept rolling getting faster as he did. His father chased him around the room as they both laughed, enjoying their father-son moment. Clara watched her boys together and smiled. "This brings back a lot of memories," Clara said as she reminisced. "You and your father used to play all the time when you were young. When he got home from work, he always wanted to chase you around the house before bed. You would always giggle and take off running when you have seen him come in through the door because you knew he was going to chase you."

Avery smiled, "That sounds like a nice memory, I wish I could remember it." Avery stopped and looked at his hands. The design in the tires impressed in his hands. He turned his hand palm up and followed the design with his pointer finger on his other hand. Just before Clara could give her "it's going to be all right speech," Christina pushed the door open and kicked a door stop in place.

"Ready to go?"

Avery nodded as Weston and Clara quickly got behind him.

"Perfect, do you need a push?" Christina walked a little further in the room as Avery spoke.

"Can."

"Great! Let's get going," Christina spun around and walked down the hall. "It's at the end here," she pointed to a huge glass door as they continued to follow her there. Avery kept wheeling himself down the hall, he was enjoying the feeling of freedom he was getting. He really felt like good things were coming his way. Christina opened the door in front of them and guided them inside. Dr. Simms was sitting on an exercise ball, bouncing, as he looked through some files that were sitting on his desk. He was an older, dark-skinned man with bright brown eyes. He was about six feet tall and had a saddened look on his face. He looked very fit for an older man but he definitely didn't seem approachable.

Christina kept the door open until the family was all inside. She released the door and walked up to the doctor's desk, "Hey, Doctor Simms, this is Avery and his family, they are very excited to be starting with you today." Avery looked around the room, not sure what to think. He was a little overwhelmed with all the equipment and gear they had around the room. He started to breathe a little heavier. Doctor Simms bounced up off of his ball and slowly walked over to the Langston family. He held out his hand, "Nice to meet you all, I'm Doctor Simms but you can call me Simms or Sim for short." Clara and Weston shook his hand and thanked him. Simms walked over to Avery in his chair and knelt down on the floor so he could look up at Avery to properly introduce himself. Avery looked down at the doctor and started breathing even heavier.

"Relax, we haven't even started therapy yet," Simms chuckled and lightly patted him on the back. Avery started to calm down after realizing the doctor wasn't such a hardass after all. Clara slowly shuffled her way over to Avery and started pushing him closer to the center of the room. There was a huge blue, mat in the middle of the floor, like the ones you see in gym class in elementary school when you were doing gymnastics. There were also other weird looking foam shapes and towels lying around on the mat. Dr. Simms pushed all the things over with his feet as he walked up to Avery in his chair. He flicked his wrist and did a few stretches on the mat. Clara and Weston looked at each other with confusion on their faces. Christina leaned over and whispered in Clara's ear, "Trust him. He knows what he's doing." Clara nodded and kept watching him stretch on the mat. Christina's beeper went off and cut the silence. She quickly pressed a button on the side of the little device, "The patient in 117 requested for you." *Beep.*

Christina replied, "Be right there." Christina quickly excused herself and left the room.

The doctor took a deep breath as she left the room. He rolled up his sleeves and placed one foam block onto the mat and another about six feet apart from the other one. He took another deep breath and walked over towards Avery, "I'm going to lift you up now." Clara and Weston stood in shock as this man easily lifted their 6 feet 6 inches son out of his chair and gently laid him onto the mat. "We are going to do some body stretches today, we have to stretch the body before we do anything." Simms laid him flat on his back and started slowly moving his legs up and down. "Ow," Avery yelled. Simms smiled and continued to move his legs. "He's hurting!" Clara responded to Avery's yelp of pain. Dr. Simms glares up at her as he kept moving his legs "He hasn't moved for over 40 days, of course, he is hurting, he needs to loosen up those muscles."

Weston nudged Clara, she quickly took a step back and nodded.

Dr. Simms continued, "How does this feel, Avery?" Avery looked up but said nothing.

"Hmmm."

Dr. Simms stood up and walked over to his desk, "Has he spoken since the accident?"

He typed a few things into his computer as Clara spoke, "Ummm. Just a few things. Like Mom, Dad, yes,noo… Just simple things."

Avery moved his head slightly to the side so he could see his mother.

"Has he moved his lips while you spoke or watch you intently as you spoke?"

Clara looked down at Avery and back at the doctor. "I feel like he understands me."

Simms nodded, "Okay, he's going to stay with me for a few hours today, and for the next two weeks, we will be working on getting him to stretch, and when he's loosened up a bit, we will start him with a little more intense work and also I am getting Tala, our speech-language pathologist, to come in as well to help Avery with his speech. He is doing amazing for the damage he sustained."

Clara and Weston nodded. "Great, thank you." Weston said, "We have high hopes for him." Doctor Simms nodded and continued typing,

"We will get him walking and talking in no time," Simms smiled at Avery and Avery smiled back.

Two weeks went by quickly, five hours a day stretching with Dr. Simms made a huge improvement on Avery's legs. He now had the strength to lift them up by himself and bend them without any help.

Dr. Simms even had him crawling a little on the mat. Avery would topple over a lot because he had no balance but at least he was moving by himself a bit.

Clara walked into the room with a coffee in one hand and a tea in the other. "Here you go, Simms, three cream and no sugar for you."

Dr. Sim hopped up off the floor and grabbed his tea, "Thank you so much."

Clara smiled and stepped back and leaned against the wall as she watched Avery try to push himself up off of his stomach. "He is really doing amazing." Dr. Sim took a sip of his tea and continued, "He started off with the brain of an infant, literally has to learn everything over and most people in his state never walk, Talk. Anything again. He is a living miracle."

Clara's eyes teared, "He was really lucky."

Dr. Sim shook his head. "There was no luck to it, God wanted him alive and that's that, I don't know how good of a connection you have with the big guy upstairs but it seems like a close one." Dr. Simms placed his tea down on his desk and went back over to Avery on the floor, pulling his hips up as Avery pushed.

"Good, good," Simms Smiled, "I'm so proud of you!"

Clara Watched as her eyes filled up, "Ummm… I'll be right back, going to bring this coffee to Weston." Simms waved his arm as she turned and left. Tears streamed down her face as she walked down the hall. She quickly pushed open the door to the public washroom and placed Weston's coffee on the counter by the sinks. She slowly sank down to the floor. And she started to sob, "God, please, give us the strength to keep going, thank you for everything you are doing for this family." Clara kept wailing as she hugged into her purse. She was completely broken, she was tired, and so overcome by emotions.

Moments later, a woman about Clara's age walked out of the bathroom stall and sat on the floor with her. She placed her hand gently on her back, "I know how you feel; sometimes, I feel like giving up. It's hard, but it will all be okay. His life will be better than ever. He will, one day, realize who he was, wasn't who he was meant to be, and he will be so much happier now than he ever was then."

Clara looked up at the beautiful stranger. She was so beautiful she almost glowed as she spoke. She was skinny with long, blonde, curly hair. Her eyes were clear and sparkled under the florescent lights but it was hard to pinpoint the color. Clara quickly stood up and brushed herself off. "I'm, I'm sorry, I didn't know anyone was in here," Clara turned to the mirror to look at her red cheeks and sad eyes. The woman stood up and pulled the paper towel out of the machine. "Here," she offered some tissue to Clara as she tilted her head in concern. Clara accepted the tissue and smiled a half smile as she blew her nose into the paper. The woman tucked her hair behind her ear and leaned over the counter, looking up at Clara as she wiped her tears, "I never use to be close to God, but when my daughter got hit by a drunk driver while driving to her exams at school, He was my only hope..."

Clara turned toward the woman as she spoke, "I prayed and thought he wouldn't give me the light of day because I was living in so much sin. But no matter what he is always here looking out for us, When we hurt, he hurts for us."

"Anyways, God knows your pain and he is here for you, everything will work out for you and your son and within time, you will look back at this moment and be amazed at how far he came. When everyone was telling you, he wasn't going to get better, he isn't going to make it, you will be able to proudly look at your son living his life better than ever. Don't worry and keep praying."

The woman patted Clara's back once again as Clara grabbed another tissue and blew her nose once again. Clara turned around, "Thanks, I really needed to hear that." The woman smiled and placed her arm around Clara. "Let's get that coffee to your husband," Clara nodded and they walked out of the bathroom together. As Clara enter into the hallway again, Weston waved as he walked toward her in the hallway. "Where have you been?" Clara smiled just in the bathroom having a chat with this beautiful woman, she really helped me. Clara turned as Weston replied, "What woman?"

Clara's eyes widened, no she was right there, "I felt her, I saw her!"

Weston scrunched up his face and looked at his wife with disbelief. "You okay?" Clara's looked all around as she gave Weston his coffee. "Yeah… I think so," Clara looked up as they started walking back to Dr. Simms, Clara was unsure of what had just happened but her faith that her son would get better have never been stronger.

Chapter 6
5th Door down

"Okay, Avery. Day 56 since your accident and look at you!" Dr. Simms shouted out across the room as Avery stood in the middle of the trampoline with a harness that attached to the ceiling. Selena, an occupational physical therapist, started jumping around Avery as he stood there. He wobbled all over as she kept jumping. It was a funny sight to see. Avery stood there 6 feet, 6 inches in height while Selena was only about 5 feet, 2 inches. She may be tiny but boy, did she make him work to stand. He wiggled and bounced more as she jumped. "Avery? Your mind seems like it is not here today. Are you nervous to start school and speech today?"

Avery hung over the trampoline and Selena jumped off and pulled the lever to gently move him from the trampoline to the mat with the steel bars on each side to practice walking. She slowly lowered him and she spoke, "Don't be scared, Mr. Ekholt, the teacher and Tala are the best we have." Avery nodded and held onto the bars as he was placed firmly on the ground. Selena stood behind Avery and helped move his legs as he pulled himself forward with his hands.

"Good!"

They did that for a full hour until Avery finished the length of the mat. Dr. Simms rolled the wheelchair over to the end of the mat next to Avery. They lowered him into the chair and detached the harness. "Good work today, Mr. Langston, very happy with you today," Simms grabbed Avery's shoulder and gave it a little squeeze to show how proud he was of him. Avery smiled as he did so.

"Hey, King Avery, you ready to go to school?" Becca pushed open the glass door as she excitedly shouted. Avery was nervous but seeing Becca made him feel a bit better. Avery wheeled himself over to Becca as he did, she watched his awe.

"Look at you! Getting stronger every day!" Becca hugged Avery as he took his hands off the wheels of the chair. He raised his hands up and hugged her back. "Let's go, Avery. See you tomorrow, Selena, Simms."

They nodded as Becca pushed Avery out the door and down the hall. They hopped into the elevator and went down to the main level. Avery had never been down there before. The elevator stopped and the big steel doors opened. Becca pushed Avery out and down another hall. The fifth door on the right was a huge door with a tiny window in it. Becca knocked. Not even 30 seconds after, a sweet, native woman with curly hair swung it open and smiled, "You must be Avery! I've heard so much about you." Avery was taken back as he heard her speak. The woman smiled again, "I'm Tala, your speech coach!" Becca pushed Avery inside the room and parked him in the front row behind a wooden desk. She bent down and locked the wheels of his chair so he wouldn't wiggle away, "I'll be back in a bit to get you."

Becca left the room as Tala pulled a chair over, "We are going to do an hour of speech therapy today, then you will have lunch. Mr. Ekholt needs you for at least two hours today to get you started on some school work."

Avery nodded like he understood what Tala was saying. He really focused when she talked. He watched her lips move as she spoke and he mimicked every lip movement. He was a great student.

"Good!"

Tala started teaching him the basics. One, two, three, A, B, C, yes, no, okay, maybe. Avery sat there for the full hour, trying to repeat everything she was saying.

As they were finishing, Mr. Ekholt walked through the door with a stack of papers in his hands. He smiled at Avery as he laid the papers down on his desk and spread them out. Tala looked up at Ekholt, then turned to Avery. "We're finished here. Your mother should be here shortly with your lunch and then you will start class with Mr. Ekholt. You are doing very well, Avery," Tala smiled and packed up her things to leave. As she left the room, Clara and Weston entered with a paper bag of food, "Here, we got you an eight-piece nugget meal. You haven't had one in a long time but I thought it would be a nice treat." Clara took everything out of the bag and flattened it on the table in front of Avery. Avery smiled as she poured the food out in front of him. The familiar scent filled his nose. Even though he couldn't remember having it before.

Weston grabbed the drinks from the drink tray and placed it on the table also. Clara and Weston both pulled chairs over and sat next to Avery as they opened their meals. Mr. Ekholt watched from afar as Avery slowly ate his food.

Clara noticed Mr. Ekholt and nudged Avery, "Eat faster, dear. We don't want to keep Mr. Ekholt waiting too long."

Avery nodded and kept eating, "No. No. Take Your time, we got all day." Mr. Ekholt replied as he looked over some of the papers, he had brought with him. Avery continued to eat his lunch as Clara starting cleaning up. "You should get to work, sweetie," Clara picked up the garbage and threw it in the nearby trash can. Weston stood up and wrapped his arm around his wife, guiding her to the door. "We will see you later, kiddo, okay?" Weston and Clara both left the room as Avery sat there in front of his cleared off desk.

Avery looked up at the teacher as he grabbed a few papers off of his desk. He also grabbed a large zip-lock bag of crayons and markers. Mr. Ekholt sat next to Avery, placing all of the things onto the desk top, "I'm Mr. Ekholt, but you can call me Andy, I'm going to help see where you're at mentally with all this school stuff." Andy slide over a little booklet in front of Avery. It had a picture of an apple on the front with a large letter "A" inside it. "This book is just to help you with your alphabet, colors, and to see if you recognize any of these things." Avery looked down at the booklet, a hint of worry cut across his face as he watched Andy take out the crayons.

"Do you know what this is?" Avery nodded as Andy pointed to the apple. "Great, now can you grab the red crayon." Andy laid out four different crayons in front of Avery. Yellow, green, blue, and red. Avery slowly slide his fingers along the crayons examining each one.

"Take your time, Avery."

Andy said as he watched Avery struggle to choose. After five minutes of staring at the crayons, Avery finally chooses the red crayon. "Great!" Andy smiled as Avery started to color the "A" inside the apple. Days went by and now Avery was learning grade two things. Basic math and spelling. Avery was doing so well. Much better than most expected of him.

By the end of the month, he could walk to his class himself, do algebra, and speak in full on sentences. Avery was progressing very well and was soon able to be released back into society.

"All your hard work is paying off, dear," Clara smiled as she watched her son get up out of bed and walk to the couch. "Yeah, I know," Avery flopped down onto the couch and turned the T.V. on. Clara flopped next to him and wrapped her arms around him, snuggling up next to him. They have never been so close in their lives.

As they snuggled watching cartoons on the T.V. Weston burst through the door with excitement all over his face.

"Shit! Weston you, scared me. What's going on?" Clara held her chest as she sat up. "I heard one of the nurses talking and they said Avery is going to get released tomorrow!" Weston jumped up and down as he spoke. He couldn't stop moving. He was just too excited. Clara stood up and hugged Weston and jumped with him, "Really? That's amazing!" Avery turned off the television and folded his hands, fiddling with his thumbs as his parents danced in glee. Weston noticed Avery sitting quietly and quickly stopped jumping, "Son, you're getting out tomorrow, what's wrong?" Avery sunk into the couch as his father and mother crowded around him. Avery swallowed and took a deep breath, "What am I going to do once I'm home?" Clara and Weston looked at each other than looked at Avery. "Well, you are going to live. Get a job, see old friends, live your life," Clara hugged him as he sighed once more. "It's all going to be okay, son." Weston patted him on the back as he went over to the drawer and started packing up their things. Just as he did, Dr. Simms Tala, Mr. Ekholt, Nurse Christina, and Nurse Becca entered the room. Everyone's heads turned to Dr. Simms as he spoke, "Well, it has been an amazing experience watching you grow into the man you are today."

Christina butted in, "We will never forget your hard work ethic and your amazing willpower. We will never underestimate a patient and what they can do because of what you showed us all these past few weeks here." Avery looked up as his mother and father sobbed in the background. "But," Mr. Ekholt chimed in, "it's time for you to go live your life. We have done all we can and now the rest is up to you."

Christina smiled with a tear in her eye, "As of tomorrow morning, you are officially released from here."

Everyone gave Avery a hug or a pat on the back as they left the room. Avery felt a mix of emotions as everyone left the room. Sadness, fear happiness, excitement, worry. He wasn't really sure what he should be feeling but I guess it was kind of exciting that he was starting a whole new chapter in his life.

Chapter 7
The New Chapter

Morning seemed to come too quickly for Avery since he was being released today. He wasn't sure how he should feel and was a little scared of what was outside waiting for him when he left. Avery watched his parents finish packing up their things and tidying the room. "Don't just sit there, Avery," Clara exclaimed cutting off Avery's train of thought. "Go do something useful like take your breakfast tray out to the cart in the hall."

Avery slowly stood up from his seat and walked over to the table where his half-eaten tray of breakfast laid. He carefully picked up the tray and slowly made his way to the hall. As he walked, he seems to concentrate very hard on his balance. He didn't want to spill what was left of his 2.5-star hospital food. Weston looked at his watch as his son made his way out of the room. "Hmm," Weston looked up at his son and back again at his watch. "He moves a little slow still, don't you think?" Weston turned his head to look at Clara folding the blankets they used the night before.

"At least, he's moving, Weston. He should speed up over time."

Weston nodded and continued watching his son as he made his way back into the room. Weston walked over to Avery and wrapped his arm around him, pulling him in close. "Ready for the drive home, bud?" Avery nodded as he stepped away from his father and grabbed his backpack. "Alright, my boys. Let's go!" Clara almost skipped as she made her way to the door to leave. Happy as a clam, Clara grabbed Weston's hand and they both walked out. Avery slowly followed them, dragging his backpack behind him. All the doctors and nurses waved goodbye as they left the building. Some even shed a tear as they watched Avery walk out of the building. His experience there changed many peoples look on other patients who suffer or will suffer from this very traumatic brain injury. Avery's story gave hope to others who had loved ones dealing with similar or the same thing.

Weston pulled the truck up to the doors of the FinRose. Clara threw her bags in the back and opened the door for Avery to sit in the front with his father. Avery took another one of his famous deep breaths and pulled himself up into the truck. Clara helped him buckle his seat belt up and closed the door. Avery looked at his feet as Clara hopped into the back seat. "All ready back here, honey," Clara tapped on the edge of Weston's drivers' seat as she spoke. Weston turned and smiled at her just before taking the truck out of park and into drive. Avery's stomach rolled as they drove off the parking lot and onto the highway. Every few seconds, Weston would take a quick look at his son as he drove, "You okay, bud?"

Weston asked Avery in a concerned tone. Clara leaned forward as much as she could with her seatbelt on and looked over at Avery as well, "You okay, sweetie?" Avery nodded, "Just feels a little weird to be moving like this."

Weston smiled and let out a large breath from his nose, "Okay, well, if you need us to stop or anything, let us know, okay?"

Weston kept going towards home as Avery replied, "Okay."

Clara leaned back into her seat and closed her eyes. Weston looked back at her through his rearview mirror and shook his head. "Didn't take long for her to pass out," Avery and Weston both laughed softly. "Maybe you should try and have a nap, too, it's going to be a long drive." Avery looked back at his mom and then out the passenger window. "Yeah, okay," Avery smiled at his father and closed his eyes. Avery's head had been pretty clear the pass week or so but for some reason, today, it was full. His head pounded as his thoughts bounced around in his head. He tried to focus on something he enjoyed but he couldn't even remember what that was, which started to frustrate him.

"Dad?" Avery looked over at his father as he drove.

"Yeah, son?" Weston focused on the road and didn't turn to respond. "What did I like before the accident?"

Avery's father sighed, "Well… I didn't know you very well before your accident, we weren't as close as we are now."

Avery sat up straighter as he listened to his father, "We weren't?"

Weston continued, "But from some of the stories I heard, you were…a lady's man, loved women, money, cars. Just things."

Avery looked out the passenger's window again as he pondered on what his father had said, "I was…m malistic. What's the word?"

"Materialistic?" Weston Added Avery nodded. "Maybe a little but like I said before, it doesn't matter who you were before, it only matters who you become now."

Avery sighed and closed his eyes once more. He couldn't remember who he truly was before but he wasn't sure he really wanted to remember. After a good 30 minutes of thinking, Avery needed to shut his brain off for a while and he fell asleep.

It seemed liked minutes but in reality, it was hours, they pulled into the driveway of their home.

Both, Avery and Clara, sleeping like a ton of bricks.

"Hey, you sleepy heads, we're home."

Clara kept snoring. Weston tried again to wake them, this time, a little louder, "Hey! We're home!"

Clara jumped as he shouted, "Weston! What the hell? Scared me half to death!"

Weston laughed, "That's why I yelled. I thought you were dead!"

Clara shook her head as Weston tried his best to hold his laughter back. Avery slowly opened his eyes and wiggled up in his seat. "We're home?" Avery turned to take his seat belt off and opened his door. He leaned out and push the door all the way open and carefully slide his body out of the truck. Clara quickly got out as well and stood next to her son, "Welcome home, Avery."

Clara patted his back as he looked mesmerized by the mansion. "This is my house?" Avery's eyes widened. Weston closed the door to his truck and walked around to

Avery, "Well, it's me and your mother's house. Our family home, you grew up here. So technically, yes." Avery lightly shook his head in confusion but carried on. Clara handed him a bag, "Here, bring this to your room." Avery started walking towards the front door. Weston ran ahead and unlocked it. Avery pushed open the door and took his shoes off. He slowly made his way over to the closet and hung his jacket up inside. Clara and Weston both watched in amazement as he seemed to remember his routine from childhood. Avery placed his backpack on a hook near the entrance and slowly walked down the large hallway. Weston and Clara followed behind him, not saying a word. Avery opened the second last door on the right and flopped onto the bed. Clara and Weston smiled.

"How did you know this was your room?" Weston asked.

"You remember?" added Clara. Avery laid there, looking up at the ceiling.

"I didn't know," Avery sighed, "but I guess I did, if that makes sense."

Weston and Clara both looked at each other.

"Maybe it's still in his mind but he can't really remember it but subliminally, he does or something," Weston concluded.

Clara nodded in agreement.

"Will you be okay for me and dad to go unpack?"

Avery also nodded, "I'll be here."

Avery stayed laying on his bed until his parents left the room. When they were gone, Avery sat up and took a good look at his childhood room. The walls were a bright green and the boards around his door and the dark hardwood flooring were pearl white. There were pictures of him playing hockey and lots of trophies and certificates. There were some from hockey, some academic awards for math and science, even some medals for being a model student. Avery kept exploring the room, hoping to unlock some memories. But everything in his room seemed to be from his teen years and not his adult life. Avery sat in a big, black leather chair that was by a desk. As he did, a sharp pain cut across his head once again. Another memory. He had seen himself sitting in his office chair waving his arms while on the phone. A half-naked woman crying as she hurried to grab her clothes up off the floor.

Avery rubbed his head as he looked down at the desk in front of him. A black laptop computer rested on the top of the desk. Avery turned in his chair and pulled the laptop open. As he did, Clara walked into the room "You okay?"

Avery nodded. "Just looking," Avery replied.

Clara rubbed his back lightly, "When you're ready, I put a few boxes of your things from your penthouse in the closet here. But there's no rush. This chair and the laptop are from your office. It's all we could get from there before the shut down."

Avery nodded and thanked his mother. She gave him a kiss on the cheek and left the room once again. Avery clicked on a few things and found a folder with a lock attached. Avery double clicked the folder. As it opened, Avery's eyes widened and he began to feel excitement in his pants. At least 40 photos of woman popped up onto the computer screen. Some had check marks on them, others did not. Avery looked through every single picture in that folder. His excitement pushed against his pants as he counted the checked off girls.

"35 checked girls? What does that even mean?" Avery kept clicking through the computer, hoping to find more information on himself. But not much else was on this computer. Besides a couple of business graphs that he had no idea how to read or what they were for. Avery pushed himself up off the chair and rolled it back into the desk. He made his way to the closet and pulled the doors open. Inside were at least five big boxes of random things from his penthouse. Avery couldn't really remember too much about his penthouse but some of the items in the boxes helped jog his memory. "I remember this. It's my journal," Avery quickly yanked the black book out of one of the boxes and sat on the edge of his bed. He quickly skimmed through the pages and came to a stop when he read these words.

"Fucked another bitch today in the penthouse shower, she was hotter than the last one. Sex has to be the best thing in the world. I can't wait to stick my dick in another chick later."

Avery shut the book and threw it on the floor, sickened at what he just read. "Was that really me?" he said aloud to himself. As he lay back onto his bed, his bedroom door creaked open. "Avery! Oh, thank God, you're home, you're okay!"

The tall athletic looking man ran across the room and gave Avery the biggest hug.

Avery looked up, "Craig?"

Craig was Avery's very good childhood friend, he used to live next door to him all growing up.

"I haven't seen you in a while man when I heard the news, I was shocked. I came to visit you a few times but you were in a coma. I haven't seen you in years man,"

Craig sat next to Avery and gave a light punch to his shoulder. Avery looked at Craig; he looked so much different from what he could remember but he knew he was a friend. Someone he knew.

"I'm sorry, apparently, I wasn't a very good friend to anyone before this accident."

Craig smiled, "No worries, pal, we made a promise when we were kids that we would always try and be there for each other and I'm here to keep that promise."

Craig stood up and grabbed a frame off the shelf. "See, this is us."

Avery reached up and gently took the frame out of Craig's hands. Avery stared at it for a few minutes. Craig sat back down next to Avery. "Do you remember when this picture was taken?" Avery shook his head. "When we were kids, we would always ride our bikes together into town, and one day, when we went, I got a flat tire and had to walk my bike home. You could have ridden home without me, could have left me, behind but you got off your bike and walked yours home, too. It was a good hour walk for sure. We carried our bikes on our shoulders for most of the trip back. You didn't have to do that but you did, so we could do it together. We talked and laughed all the way home. When we got home, you grabbed your mother's camera and asked her to take our picture because we just came from a long journey. We both were so sore the next day, carrying our bikes on our shoulders wasn't the best idea."

Craig smirked as he looked at the picture again. Avery nodded and laughed, "I actually do remember some of this story, we went to go get ice cream from the new shop in town at the time."

Craig nodded, "Yeah, exactly!"

Avery smiled, "Was that before or after you dragged me behind your quad while I was wearing my rollerblades, I got for passing my final exam?"

Craig laughed, "Oh, I almost forgot about that! Those were some fun times."

Both Craig and Avery laughed as they reminisced about their past. After a good hour of laughing and chatting, Craig stood up off the bed, "I got to run, man, there's a guy down the street who needs me to re-shingle his house and I told him I'd start today, but we will definitely catch up later, okay?"

Craig gave Avery another hug and left the room. Avery smiled from ear to ear. Craig's visit gave him hope for his future.

Craig came and visited Avery every day for two full years. In those two years, Avery progressed greatly. He went to school, worked a side job at the local ski hill, and became a volunteer firefighter. Avery took two years to focus on himself. Not worried about who he was but who he was becoming. Avery's personality changed drastically. He was a whole new man. Before he only cared about himself and what he could gain from a situation, now he cared about helping others at any cost. He was finally the person he wanted to be and his parents couldn't be prouder. The only thing that seemed to be lingering from his accident was a small limp in his walk. But that didn't stop him from doing everything in his power to better himself. Avery seemed to almost have it all again. Even though he didn't have lots of his own money or a fancy car, he felt complete. Well, almost complete.

Chapter 8
The Search

"Come on, Avery, just sign up!" Craig pushed the laptop towards Avery and Avery pushed it right back. "No, I'm not ready." Craig took the computer off the desk and brought it over to the bed.

"Well, get ready," Craig continued to scroll down the page on the dating site. "Single. Male. You are about 6'4", right?" Craig began to slowly type in the information. Craig wasn't great with computers but he could get the job done.

"I'm 6'6"." Avery added.

Craig backspaced and re-typed his height.

"Now would you consider yourself average looking, Okay I guess, Sexy or extremely sexy? Let's go with extremely sexy," Craig joked as Avery shook his head.

"Just average."

Craig nodded, "Sexy it is."

They both laughed as they continued to finish the dating profile online.

"All done."

Craig submitted the profile and turned the laptop towards Avery. Avery got up off the chair and walked over to the bed, sitting on the edge looking down at the screen.

"So, to look at girls, you click here and then you can read their profiles, then over here is if you want to message them and over here is where you check your incoming messages."

Avery took a deep breath, "I don't know about this, man, seems kind of sketchy."

Craig smiled, "This will be good practice to get yourself back out there. Here, pass me your phone."

Avery hesitated but after some quick thinking, gave him the phone anyways. Craig downloaded the dating app on his phone and gave it back to him.

"Just talk to someone you think is attractive and see what happens. You were a real lady's man back in the day and I doubt that has changed so get in there."

Avery walked over to his closet and grabbed his fireman's Jacket and pulled it on, "I'll look later I got a meeting at the fire hall in 20 minutes I got to get going." Craig and Avery said their see you laters and both went on their way.

By this time now, Avery had gotten his license renewed and was driving a black Silverado. After his accident most, people thought he would be too nervous to get back behind the wheel again but not Avery. Avery loved driving, he found that driving was a great escape from his everyday stresses and it was a great way to go get his fast-food he loved. Avery would eat fast-food almost every day, you wouldn't be able to tell just by looking at him though, he was a fit man. He could eat eight burgers a day and never gain a pound. Avery was a special case, he may not of thought so but he was a lucky man. According to most doctors, he should have been dead. Not working as a firefighter, eating burgers, and joining dating sites, that's for sure. Some doctors even called his case the "God's Written Miracle," which meant they thought God kept him alive because Avery wasn't done with God's plan yet. They say God has a plan for everyone already written and this was just a speed bump in Avery's story to lead him to where he needed to go. Avery had a bigger purpose and he will find out what that is soon but right now, let's get back to the story.

After the meeting, Avery came home to an empty house. He walked into the kitchen and turned on the coffee maker to brew himself a cup of Joe before sitting down to relax and watch some television. As he walked towards the coffee cups, Avery noticed a piece of paper on the counter. It read *"Avery, Me and your father are gone on our cruise, we will be back in two weeks. Please be safe and take care of the house while we are away. Don't forget to mow the lawn and water the flowers please. Love mom and dad."*

Avery picked up the note off the counter and stuck it to the fridge with a magnet. Avery mixed his coffee and continued his way into the living room, slowly walking to make sure his coffee wouldn't spill. Even after two years, he still would concentrate all his energy on not spilling as he walked.

He slowly placed his mug on the side table and sat in the recliner, facing the T.V. Avery pulled the lever up and as he did, the recliner foot rest popped up. Avery took a moment to enjoy the comfort of the chair before grabbing his coffee for a sip. He placed the cup back onto the table and leaned to the right to slide his phone out of his jeans pocket. He pressed the power button.

"Six notifications."

All from the dating app. Avery smiled and pressed the app. As he did it opened, and showed an envelope flashing red. Avery tapped on the envelope and started to read the messages "No…no… Wait," Avery spoke to himself aloud as he inspected the messages. Avery's cock quickly bulged as he read the third message in his inbox. "Hey, sexy, love your pic, I'm free tonight, want to fuck?" Avery quickly responded with his address and a wink face. Not too long after, there was a soft knock on the door. Avery quickly ran to open it. As he did, the cold winter wind filled the entrance.

"Are you Lifesizedteddybear?"

Avery nodded vigorously.

"I'm BigBoobedBeth, nice to meet you."

They both quickly embraced and started roughly started making out. She jumped into his arms as he carried her into his room. He pushed her against the wall as he tried to wiggle out of his pants. Beth yanked off her top exposing her bare breast in his face. Even though Avery haven't done anything like this in years, it felt natural too him. He quickly got back into the groove of things. Beth leaned her head back in pleasure as Avery slammed his hard cock deep inside her. Avery leaned down and placed his mouth around her nipple and started flicking it with his tongue as he continued to ram his member inside her. Moments later, they both came. Avery laid down onto his bed and patted the edge.

"Come lay down."

Beth shook her head and giggled, "I don't cuddle, I just fuck. Thanks for the great time."

Beth picked up her clothing and went on her way. Avery sat in his bed, feeling a feeling he had never felt before. He felt used and lonely. He really enjoyed sex but this time, it wasn't enough. He wanted more. Avery got up and put his boxers on and made his way out to the living room. He sat back into the recliner and turned the television back on. "I guess that's number 36," he sighed. Avery felt low, lower than he had ever remembered feeling before. For the first time in Avery's life, the number wasn't a trophy or an accomplishment, it was just a number. Avery wanted more than just sex; he was ready for love.

Chapter 9
Winter Is Coming

Winter quickly slammed the door behind her as she entered her family home. She booked it down over the stairs and opened the door of her bedroom. She flung her work bag across the room and flopped onto the bed face first letting her legs dangle over. As she laid there, her little, Corgi puppy, Coby, jumped up onto the bed and licked her face, "Oh, buddy, I'm so glad it's the weekend." Winter rubbed his belly as she vented about her day. She stood up and looked in the mirror. She hated looking at herself in the mirror. She had little hairs on her face which when she seen it, made her feel insecure and ugly. She quickly fixed her hair and turned away from the mirror. She bent over and dragged her work bag over as she looked for her cell phone. She slides the unlock button on her phone and tapped on her text messages. She read "Coming over for the weekend, lucky?"

A huge smile cut across her face as she read the text from her boyfriend, Mark. Lucky was the nickname he gave her because on their first date about ten months ago; after dinner, they went to the local casino and he won big on one of the machines. He considered her his good luck charm. She replied instantly.

"Sounds good, be over in 30."

Winter grabbed a backpack and filled it with clothes and whatever else you bring when you go for a sleepover. She also grabbed a small envelope out of the closet and put it in the pack as well. It was her good friend's birthday today and the party was later tonight. Being excited she hurried up the stairs and grabbed a bottle of cheap wine she bought the day before to take with her. As she stuffed the bottle into her, bag her mother came through the door. "Oh, you're home? How was work?" Winter's mother kicked off her shoes and slowly made her way up the stairs and gave her daughter a kiss. "Heading over Marks?"

Winter smiled and nodded, "Going for the weekend, I'll see you on Sunday night, okay? Love you."

Winter kissed her mother back and quickly headed out the door. His house was only about a 15–20-minute walk away so when it was nice out. Winter would always walk instead of taking the bus or driving. After working a long day sitting at a desk, dealing with a witch of a boss and client phone calls, she really enjoyed the fresh air and moving her legs.

Now you may be wondering who is this girl? Why are we randomly here and not with Avery? She seems happy, why are we even talking about her? Well…just bear with me, it will all come together soon.

Winter finally arrived at Marks house and softly knocked on the door. As soon as she did, Mark yanked the door open and grabbed her arm pulling her inside, "You said 30mins…it's been 45."

Mark stood there staring down at Winter as she pulled her arm back gently as she took off her backpack and unzipped her jacket. She laughed softly as she starred back up at his serious face, "It was only a few minutes later than I said. You must have missed me."

She hugged into him as he shut the door behind them.

He grabbed her bag and brought it downstairs into his bedroom and placed it onto the chair beside his bed. Winter sat on the edge of the bed as Mark walked over to his mini fridge and grabbed a beer. Mark drank a lot. When he wasn't working, he was drinking. Winter didn't really like it when he was drunk but she loved him, so she put up with it.

"Try not to drink too much, okay? We have Holly's party in a few hours."

Mark sighed and popped open his bottle of bud, "I just want to stay home tonight, watch hockey and order a pizza."

Mark moved the backpack that was sitting on the chair and flopped into his throne. That's what he would call it anyway. He was the king.

"But you promised you would go with me," Winter's face turned into a frown. Mark stood up quick and started speaking in an angry tone, "I worked all day I don't want to go anywhere; this is bullshit." He sat next to her on the bed as he kept venting angrily. Winter shifted closer to the edge, a little nervous, "I'll go by myself, it's okay." Winter looked over at him concerned, very confused, never seeing him like this before. Mark suddenly swung his arm and hit Winter right in the face, knocking her onto the floor. "Ow!" Winter grabbed her face quickly with her jaw opened and her eyes widen. Mark quickly knelt down on the floor, "Oh, shit, I'm so, so sorry, I didn't mean to do that. Are you okay? It was an accident. I didn't mean to hurt you. I'll go to the party with you. I said I would. I'm sorry, I will never hurt you again, I promise… Let's get ready."

Mark hugged her tight as she sat there in confusion, trying to figure out what the hell just happened.

"Ahh yeah, it's okay. Let's get ready, I'll call a cab."

Mark jumped up off the floor and walked over to his closet, picking out clothing to wear. Winter stood up slowly, brushing herself off. It was an accident after all. The cab came and Mark opened the door for her as she stepped inside. They sat holding hands in the back of the cab until they reached their destination. Mark paid for the cab like a gentleman and helped Winter out. Holly and her friends were already in the garage partying and half drunk. "Winter!" Holly ran over and gave Winter the biggest hug. "Happy birthday, hun!" Winter squeezed back as they headed to the garage. Winter pointed back at Mark as they all walked forwards.

"That's Mark, my boyfriend."

"Oh, I know Mark, he used to date a coworker I worked with for a little bit."

"Oh cool!" Winter replied as Holly dragged her into the garage. Winter grabbed the card out of her purse and placed it on the gift table. She then walked over to the cooler and grabbed a drink. Mark came up behind her and whispered in her ear, "Drink as much as you want, you're staying at my place, so no worries." Winter nodded and continued pouring her drink. Mark walked outside with the other girls' boyfriends and sat by the fire drinking another bud. After a few drinks, Winter, Holly, and some other girls were laughing and having fun.

"I need to pee, come with me, Winter, please," Holly shouted as she started making her way to the house on the other side of the property.

"I'm coming, wouldn't want your ass to fall in."

They both laughed and went inside. Holly pulled Winter aside to the kitchen. She pushed some of the random things on the counter over and she hopped onto the countertop, swinging her feet as she sat. "Are you okay?" Holly placed her hand on her shoulder as she asked.

"Yeah, I'm good, why?" Winter took a step back as Holly swung her feet.

"I heard some things about Mark but I have no idea if they are true. My co-worker told me; she was pretty upset at the time so it could be just bullshit."

Holly slides off the counter and opened the fridge as she spoke, "She said he used to be pretty verbally abusive to her or something like that. So, I'm just checking up on you."

Winter shook her head, "No, no, he's great."

Holly smiled as she closed the fridge and grabbed a container of cut up fruit. She popped off the lid and made her way to the front door. "Okay, as long as you're okay. I didn't really need to pee," Holly laughed as she made her way outside. Winter stood on the deck, looking over at Mark talking with the guys and Holly's mom. Drinking what looked like to be his tenth beer. Winter shook her head once more and walked over to the fire where everyone now was.

"Hey, it's getting late and we worked all day, I think I'm ready for bed," Winter softly stated as she lightly nudged Mark.

"Ahhhhhhh, one more beer then we can go."

Winter nodded and lightly rubbed his back as she made her way to the garage to call a cab in a quiet space. Just as she hung up her phone, Mark grabbed her hips pulling her into him, "Hey, babe, I'm ready now."

Winter laughed, "okay, okay, simmer down. The cab will be here shortly, let's go wait by the road."

Mark agreed and grabbed her hand and held it tight, maybe a little too tight but he was drunk, he didn't mean to. Winter walked over to Holly and gave her a hug, "We're taking off but thanks for having us."

Holly smiled and hugged back, "No problem, thanks for coming!" Mark tugged Winter's jacket and she said goodbye to Holly.

"I'm coming, relax."

Mark pulled Winter closer and forcefully guided her away from the crowd.

"Hey, I can walk by myself just fine, thanks."

Winter pushed Mark off of her side. Mark didn't like that, he quickly grabbed her arm and twisted it behind her back, "I want to make sure u get in the cab safe, you have been drinking." He tightens up his grip as the cab stopped in front of the house. Winter walked as Mark kept pushing her arm into her back.

"Stop, it hurts."

Mark let go and opened the cab door.

"Get in."

Winter ducked her head as she shuffled her way into the van. They closed the door and gave the driver the address. "Hey, can you stop at the next liquor store that comes up, please?" Mark leaned back and wrapped his arm around Winter as the driver nodded, "No problem, buddy, there's one just up the street."

Mark quickly slid his arm off of winter and scooched over close to the door, holding the handle, getting ready to hop out. The driver pulled over and parked in front of the store. The lights shined into the van, making a glow appear over the cab driver's head.

"I'll be right back, babe," Mark slid the door open and lightly slid it where it was closed but not completely hitched. The cab driver looked into his rearview mirror, staring at Winter. Winter shifted over closer to the window feeling a little uncomfortable as she noticed his off-putting stare. He smiled at her while he glared at the mirror. "Would you ever cheat on your boyfriend?" the cab driver said is a dark deep voice. Winter was taken aback as her jaw dropped once again. "Are you serious?" Winter started to shuffle her way to the door.

"You are exactly what I'd like to have right now," the cab driver stated. Winter grabbed for the door handle and as she did, Mark hopped back into the cab with a 24 pack of beer. "All right, let's go," Mark flopped his beer onto the floor and slammed the door shut. Winter sat back in the seat and didn't say a word. Mark looked over at her with concerned eyes, "You okay?" Winter shook her head as Mark pried at her to tell him what's up. "Here ya go," the cab parked in front of Marks house with his emergency lights flashing, "Here's the money, keep the change."

Winter threw $40 at him as she quickly squeezed her way around Mark and out of the cab. Mark rushed behind her, slamming the door. He ran up to Winter, grabbing her by the shoulders aggressively shaking her, "What the hell is wrong?"

The cab driver was hitting on me and it made me uncomfortable. Mark instantly filled with rage as the cab driver drove off. He ran after the cab, waving his arms in the air. Shouting random curses at him. "Hey, stop it, stop it. He's just some idiot," Winter placed her hand on his back as he stopped to catch his breath. "What a dick, you're mine and he knew that!" Mark swatted Winter's hand off of him as he stomped his way back down the street towards his house. "Come on!" Mark shouted. Winter quickly ran behind him like an obedient puppy following her master's commands. Mark stumbled up the stairs as Winter grabbed his house keys and unlocked the door, "Here, hun, let me help you with your shoes." Winter bent down on the floor as Mark leaned against the wall, lifting one foot at a time for Winter to take his shoes off. Mark grabbed her ponytail and yanked her up off the floor and pulled her in for a kiss. "Ouch! Don't do that, it hurts," Winter grabbed her ponytail and yank it out of his hands.

"Let's go to bed, you need a glass of water and a good nap," Mark stumbled across the floor and down the stairs, leaning his weight on Winter as she pushed against him helping him stand up straight. Winter kicked open the bedroom door as she did Mark pushed her out of the way and collapsed onto his bed. He quickly turned onto his back and fixed his pillow behind his head. "Here, drink this," Winter grabbed a bottle of water from the fridge and opened the cap. As she brought it close to his mouth, Mark shouted, "I don't need water!" as he did, he knocked the water right out of Winter's hands and onto the floor.

"Oh, shit, Mark! You're too drunk to handle right now," Winter grabbed a towel from the dirty laundry basket and started to soak up the water. Mark softly started to mumble. "What is it, hun?" Winter stood up throwing the towel back into the basket. Mark mumbled once again.

"'Ere."

"Come here."

Winter walked up to Mark as he laid on the bed and bent down closer to his face so she could hear what he was saying. As she did, Mark grabbed her shirt and pulled as hard as he could, pulling her down on top of him.

"Stop it, Mark, you're going to tear my shirt! This is not funny."

Winter tried to push herself up off him as he kept yanking her shirt.

"I never said this was funny," Mark slurred as he ripped her shirt off of her and slide his hand under her bra. "This will do," Mark smirked as he did.

Winter pushed him back with her feet as she sat up, "Stop it! You're drunk!"

She quickly grabbed her shirt and started to wiggle her way off the mattress. Mark, not saying a word, grabbed her tightly and pinched each arm as hard as he could, making Winter jerk back and hit her head off the wall.

"Ow, you're hurting me!"

Mark dead weighted his body on top of her chest and face as he ripped her pants off and threw them onto the floor. Winter tried pushing him off but her arms were trapped under the weight of his body. He quickly readjusted himself, pinning her arms down to her sides as he slides on a condom that he had in his pocket. He forced his member inside of her as she cried. When he was finished, he flopped over onto his side and turned into her and cuddled her as he snored. Winter turned into the wall and cried. She couldn't move, she was in pain, she was hurt and his arms were tightly wrapped around her, where she couldn't even breathe if she moved a certain way. She laid there staring at the white wall in front of her feeling empty. Her thoughts racing in her head, *He was drunk, don't take it personally. He loves you, that's why he wanted to have sex. He was just upset about the cab driver. He didn't know what he was doing. I deserved it; I wasn't being a very good girlfriend. I shouldn't have given him water. I should have known better.*

Winter closed her eyes and eventually fell asleep. She woke up the next morning with her clothes folded on the chair beside the bed neatly and a bottle of water next to it. Winter looked around the room in confusion, wondering where Mark was. She scanned the room looking for her cell phone, which was nowhere in sight. She quickly pulled on her clothes and slowly peeped around the door.

"Mark?" Winter quickly grabbed her stuff and ran upstairs to the bathroom. She fixed her hair and brushed her teeth. Just as she was finishing, she heard a door being shut. "Hey, u awake yet, lazy?" Mark shouted across the house as he did.

Winter popped her head out of the bathroom door, "Yeah, I'm here."

Mark walked up to her and kissed her, "Awesome, I got something for you." Winter tilted her head and took a step back into the bathroom. Mark put his hand out for her to hold. Winter lightly placed her hand in his and he guided her into the kitchen. As he did, she noticed her phone sticking out of his pant pocket. He grabbed a tray of ice cubes and a bottle of hot sauce out of the fridge. He placed them on the counter and smiled at Winter.

"Ummm… What are you doing?"

Mark laughed, "Don't worry, just trust me."

He pinned her body against the cabinets and poured hot sauce onto his thumb and pointer finger, "Don't move." Winter leaned back as far as she could as Mark pushed his fingers right up to her nostrils, making her eyes water and her nose burn. Winter pushed him off of her as she coughed and tried to catch her breath.

"What the hell, Mark?" Mark pushed back into her, grinding his hard cock up against her leg.

Winter's eyes welled with tears; she couldn't even open her eyes to see what he was going to do next. He cuffed her hands together behind her back and dragged her to the couch that sat in the living room. Tears fell from her eyes as he stuffed socks in her mouth. He held his hand over her mouth, so she was forced to breathe from her burning nose. He quickly took three ice cubes out and covered them in a paper towel, dipping them in the water, he had in the glass next to them. Making it super wet and cold. He shoved the cold ice to her burning nose which made it burn worse and also made it harder to breathe. He yanked the socks out of her mouth as she screamed in pain.

"You don't like that, Wolverine?" That was also another nickname he had for her when he was upset. He knew she hated the little hairs on her face and he made sure she felt bad about them every chance he could.

He unlocked the cuffs, letting her hands-free, he pushed her down flat on the couch and cleaned up the area around them. Walking back into the kitchen. She sat up and forced her eyes open, pushing the handcuff off the couch and onto the floor. She rubbed her nose with the sleeve of her sweater and Mark watched her from the kitchen. Winter sat there, in tears, embarrassed and slightly scared of what was going to happen next. She felt trapped, "You promised you would never hurt me again." Winter struggled to speak. Mark walked out from the kitchen and stood in front of Winter, looking down at her as he lifted her chin up with his right hand, "Promises don't mean anything." He squeezed her chin tighter, just before letting it go. He turned to the window and opened the blinds so the sun could shine into the house.

"My father died when I was young. Family friends and actual family promised to take me fishing, teach me how to fix a car, help me be a man. But that didn't happen, they broke their promises. They all said shit to make themselves feel better about me losing my father but never came through on anything."

Winter slowly pushed herself up on the couch and walked over to Mark, she wrapped her arms around his waist, "I'm sorry, Mark, that must have really hurt you."

Mark started to tear up, "It did, but I grew up to be fine without them. Without a father, I don't need anyone." Mark lightly lifted Winter's arms off of him and sat on the couch and turned the hockey game on. Winter stood there wondering what to do next. She felt bad for him, but that still didn't give him an excuse to do what he did. Mark quickly fell asleep on the couch. When Winter was sure, he was really asleep, she slid her phone out of his pocket and quickly ran out of his house. She just wanted to go home.

When Winter arrived at home, she quickly closed and locked the door, threw her boots and jacket off, and ran downstairs to her room. Luckily, her parents weren't home to pester her with questions of how was her night. As she entered her bedroom, her sweet corgi pup, Coby, chased after her. He always missed her when she was away.

"Hey, buddy," Winter bent over to pick him up off the floor and placed him gently onto her bed. She laid next to him and cuddle into his furry back and started to cry. Coby never moved, he just laid there and comforted her. Winter felt alone, her parents were always working or gone camping, she felt like she never had anyone to talk to. Except for her best friend, Aaron. He lived in another province but they always tried to be there for each other the best way they could.

As she cried, her phone rang, a little nervous to look thinking it may be Mark noticing she had left, she slowly flipped over her phone to read the caller ID.

"Best Friend"

"Oh, thank God," Winter sighed with relief as she picked up. "Aaron! Just who I needed to talk to."

Aaron replied, "Hey, babe! What's up?"

Winter rolled over onto her back, "It's like you knew I needed to talk with you right now."

Aaron laughed, "Hahaha. You know how we are connected, I told you this."

Winter smiled and started to cry, "I really miss you, Aaron, I need you."

"What's up babe, what did that prick do to you this time?" Winter explained to Aaron about everything that had happened with Mark. After two hours of crying, laughing, and crying, some more Aaron laid down the law, "Listen, honey, you need to stop seeing this asshole. He is bad news, there's something messed up about this guy and you're lucky you got out of the alive, he could have murdered you or something. Like break it off with this freak and in five more months, we will be together again when you come visit."

Winter nodded, "Mmhmmm, I know, you're right. I just thought he loved me."

Aaron replied in a soft tone, "Oh, Winter, if he loved you, he wouldn't hurt you like he does. He's crazy babe, you need to tell someone, like a cop or some shit."

Winter sighed, "I'm just going to forget about it."

Aaron yawned as he replied one last time, "Now, you go get some rest, I got class in four hours so I'm going to try to get some z's but I'll call you later, okay, boo?"

Winter said her good byes and hung up the phone. She leaned over the bed and plugged her phone into the charger already plugged into the wall.

I need some rest, she thought to herself as she laid back onto her pillow and closed her eyes.

She woke up forty minutes later to her phone buzzing and ringing like a mad man. She rubbed her eyes and quickly turned over to grab her phone. She yanked the charger and unplugged it as she checked her missed messages and calls. Eight missed calls and 13 text messages.

"Mark"

"Mark"

"Mark"

All from Mark.

Where did you go babe?

Babe?

Where are you?

Winter?

ANWSER ME!

Where the fuck are you?

Whatever, fucking leave me just like everyone else. You won't stay away from me for long anyways, I took your V card and they are always clingy after that.

You left your necklace here; you have to come over to get it back.

Reply to me. Damn it!

W.T.F. Winter!

Don't make me mad again, call me now!

Winter shook as she read the messages. She sat there debating whether to call or just text him the break up. "I don't owe him anything!" she yelled out to herself.

Winter texted "*Don't ever text me again. I really loved you but you treat me like crap. It's over, Mark.*"

Winter threw her phone onto the floor and started to cry. Just as she threw her phone, it started to ring.

It's just Mark, don't pick up.

Or maybe its Mom or Dad…they are traveling, maybe I should check. Something may have happened.

Winter got up out of bed and picked her phone up off the floor.

"Missed call from Tay, Tay"

"Ahhh, Taylor, I better call her back."

Before she even got a chance, Taylor calls back again.

"Hey, winner!" Taylor yells out over the phone.

"I miss you, gurl, you should totally come to my house tonight for some drinks."

Winter sighs, "Me and Mark broke up so I could use a drink."

"Oh my God, Winner. I'm sorry, you know what, my boyfriend's friend, Justin, is coming here tonight too and he only lives a little away from you I'll get him to pick you up and you can stay here tonight in the spare room. Just chill and have fun, no worries, I got u, boo, I'm going to call Justin now and I'll see you in a bit, okay?" Taylor hangs up the phone before Winter could even reply. Winter shakes her head and smiles at her phone.

"Oh, Taylor."

Taylor was one of Winter's best friends. She met her at work two years ago and they have been friends ever since. They were two total opposites but they both leveled each other out. Taylor was a hardworking, party gal and Winter was a soft hearted, kept to herself, play it safe gal. Even though they were so different, they got along so well.

Winter quickly got up, packed a small bag, and let her dog out to pee before Justin arrived in his shitty dodge truck. It was red and rusted, and even though it was the middle of December, this thing had no winter tires or even a back window for that matter. It was covered in duct tape and cheap plastic wrap. But, hey, it worked. Winter locked the door and made her way out to the little two-seater truck. "Hey there, beautiful, you need a ride?" Justin smiled as he leaned over to open the door from the inside. Winter pulled the door further open and flopped into the passenger seat, "Thanks, Justin, I really needed a drink tonight." Winter placed her overnight bag between her feet on the floor as she yanked the seatbelt across her body and clipped it in. Justin pulled out of the driveway and onto the road as they chatted. "Rough day?" he asked as he turned his signal light on to go right.

"You could say that." Winter sighed, "Long story short, I broke it off with my jack ass boyfriend of a year." Winter leaned down and grabbed a bottle of water out of her bag and took a sip. "Oh, I'm sorry. He will regret it," Justin quickly looked over and lightly squeezed her hand and placed it back onto the steering wheel. "Thanks," Winter twisted the cap back onto the bottle and stuffed it into her bag again. They sat in silence the rest of the way to Taylor's house.

When they arrived, Justin quickly parked and jumped out of the truck racing his way over to open the door for Winter before she got a chance to do it herself.

"I can open my own door, silly."

"But, thanks."

Justin blushed and nodded as he led her into the house.

"Winner!" Taylor shouted across the room already drunk.

"Hey!" Winter shouted back as they embraced. "Before you drink the amazing drink I mixed for you, we need to take a hit and talk about all this bullshit."

Taylor grabbed her purse and pulled out a green pipe she had placed inside. Taylor was a pretty girl, she had long, beautiful brown hair and a natural beauty about her. She was definitely born in the wrong time zone since she looked and smelled like a 60s-70s babe. Pro love, pro weed, pro peace. She was a breath of fresh air.

Taylor dragged Winter outside the house and out onto the patio. She sat down at the table and started to fill her bowl with beautiful top-grade green.

"So, what the fuck did he do?" Taylor lit the bowl and quickly placed her finger on the choke and sucked.

"Just a lot of shit, I'm just done with him," Taylor sucked in the smoke and held it, passing the pipe to Winter. Winter took in the smoke and held it as Taylor let hers out.

"Yeah, screw him. Let's just have a fun night with some good friends," Winter nodded as let out the smoke.

After a few puffs of the good stuff, they both were high and feeling good and walked back inside. Justin and Ben (Taylor's boyfriend) were standing in the corner of the room chatting and drinking. Taylor and Winter started drinking their drinks and laughing. Not sure at what but whatever it was it was funny.

"Man, I feel bad for Winter, she doesn't deserve to be with assholes. She's such a good girl," Ben whispered to Justin as they looked over at the girls laughing and drinking.

"She sure is beautiful," Justin took another gulp of his beer as he starred at winter from the other side of the room. Ben smiled, "You should totally try and get with her man. You guys would be perfect together." Ben finished his beer and grabs another from the fridge beside them. Justin quickly downed the rest of his to catch up with Ben.

“Yeah, I’mma go talk to her,” Justin downed another beer.

“Liquid courage?” Ben laughed.

“Exactly,” Justin nodded as he stumbled his way over across the room. By this time, everyone was pretty drunk and having a good time. Justin leaned against the wall next to Winter. They both had been laughing, drinking, and chatting for about an hour. “I just want to kiss you,” Justin admitted. Winter, drunk and dazed, grabbed his face and starting making out with him.

Ben and Taylor now cuddled on the couch together drunk, laughed at them, “Oh my God, ha-ha, that’s great.” Ben laughed as he nudged Taylor to look. Taylor stumbled her way over to Winter and tapped her on the shoulder as she and Justin were making out, “Hey, Hey, hay! I’m going to bed. You can stay up as long as u want, you know where the spare room is. Night.”

Taylor made her way up over the stairs and into her room.

Winter sat up as Justin leaned in for another kissed. Winter quickly held out her arms to deny him of the kiss. Ben walked over and sat next to Justin.

“Ugh, I think I need to… Ummm… goo to ah, bread, bed.”

Winter slurred her words as she spoke. She had never been this drunk before. She stumbled over her own feet and fell on her knees. Ben and Justin quickly ran over and picked her up off the floor.

“Hey, you can’t walk down over those stairs by yourself we will help ya down.”

Ben grabbed Winter tightly as he titled his head towards her to signal Justin to grab her, too. Justin quickly understood and wrapped his arm around her waist. They guided her to the spare room in the basement.

"There, you stay here and Justin, you can sleep on the couch in the family room. Night."

Ben turned the light on and left the room, making his way upstairs to Taylor.

"Justin, I'm so drunk."

Winter stumbled over to the bed and took off her socks and her shirt.

She was now standing in front of Justin in just a bra and yoga pants. She quickly flopped down on the bed. Justin stood there watching her every move.

"Justin, you don't have to sleep on the couch, you can sleep on the bed, it's big enough for us both."

Winter covered up and turned on her side half passed out. Justin's eyes widened as he quickly took off his clothes and turned the lights off. He slid into bed and leaned over cuddling into Winter's back.

"Can you… Can you…shift over please," Justin wiggled over even closer to Winter Sliding his hand down her back and around her hips sliding it into her pants, feeling around for her clit.

"No…no, stop."

Winter very drunk, very weak tries to squirm out of his grasp.

"Shhh…" Justin whispers. Winter quickly gives up as Justin continues to finger her. He grabs her hand and forces in onto his member. Winter shortly after passes out completely as Justin continues to take advantage of her state.

The next morning, a light knock on the spare room door wakes Winter. She rubs her eyes and holds her head in her hands as she tries to focus on the figures standing in front of her.

"Morning, you two."

Breakfast is ready. Taylor and Ben smile and nudge each other as they turn to go back upstairs. Justin quickly gets up and pulls his pants and shirt back on,

"Yum, breakfast!" Justin pulls his socks back on and leaves the room making his way to the kitchen for breakfast. Winter sits up in the bed, confused and drained. Her head spinning in more than one way. Apparently, alcohol, weed, and sadness don't mix. Winter pulled her clothing back on and made her way to the bathroom. She closes and locks the door behind her as she turns on the sink and splashes her face with cold water. She looks at herself in the mirror with disgust. She then pukes into the sink and quickly rinses it. Her body aches as she lifts the toilet sit up to go pee. As she sits, her vagina throbs in pain. As she pees, she slowly recalls moments from last night.

"Oh God."

She quickly stands up and leans over the toilet to puke once again. Winter can't fully recall everything from the night before but she for sure doesn't feel good about it.

Winter slowly makes her way up over the stairs and scuffs her way to the fridge to grab a glass of water. Everyone sat around the table, eating breakfast was laughing and smiling.

"You okay. Huh?" Taylor asks with a mouth full of bacon. Winter nodded, "Heard ya, puking your guts up. Must have had some fun last night."

Ben joked as he drank his milk. Justin hid his face in his toast as Winter replied.

"I think I'm just going to drink this water and sit for a minute."

Winter looked at her phone two missed messages from her father.

"We're home. Where are you, sweetheart?" Winter responded.

"At Taylors. Hey, can you come get me please?"

A few minutes later, Winter's dad responded, *"On the way."*

Winter's dad never questioned Winter when she asked for a ride or help. He just got in the jeep and got her. He was good that way.

"Well, I better get going, got to do something's today before work tomorrow. Need a ride, Winter?"

Justin asked as he put his plate in the sink, "No, I'm good…"

Winter held in an urge to puke as he asked, "Alright then, see you guys."

Everyone waved goodbye as Justin left.

"You okay?" Taylor asked one more time. Winter shook her head. "I don't think so. I'm just going to go home, my dad's coming to get me."

Winter stood up and grabbed her bag. Taylor stood up and gave her a hug.

"Okay, hun, if you need anything let me know."

Winter nodded and grabbed her shoes and walked out of the house. Winter started to walk towards home as she did her father pulled up the driveway like a maniac. Winter smiled with relief and jumped inside.

"Rough time or what'?" Winter's father asks as he spins around and speeds off.

"Well, me and Mark broke up." Winter's dad smiled and quickly turned it into a frown.

"Oh… I never liked him anyway."

Winter shook her head as her father drove them both home.

When they arrived home, Winter slowly pushed open the door to their lime green jeep and slide out the slide onto the garage floor. She walked towards the inside door as the huge metal garage door started to close behind her.

"Thanks for the ride, Dad."

Winter softly said as she started to take off her winter boots. Her father lite a cigarette and took a quick puff.

"Any time, my girl."

Winter shuffled her way inside and quickly made her way downstairs to her bedroom once again. Coby was there, lying on her bed, waiting for her to come home for cuddles. Winter smiled as she seen her cute Corgi pups' ears raise as she walked into the room. Coby always made her smile. He was truly her best friend. He was always there for her when she needed him and he was always so happy to see her, plus he was a great listener and an even better cuddle buddy.

Winter flopped down on the bed once again as she did Coby wiggled his way up to her face and started licking her like he hadn't seen her in years, "Ha-ha, relax, boy… I'm home...ha-ha." Winter giggled as Coby kept licking her face.

"Okay... Okay...that's enough boy. ha-ha."

Coby simmered down and rooted his nose at her arm so she would cuddle into him. He was a big baby and Winter loved it.

Winter laid there with her eyes closed as she snuggled into Coby. His warm body comforted her as she dwelled in thoughts of the night before. Winter's thoughts were bouncing around in her head like they were on a trampoline. "Just forget it, maybe it wasn't such a big deal. I was so drunk... I'll just be more careful next time...lesson learned. Mistakes are just lessons, right?"

Winter sighed again as she slowly drifted off to sleep. She woke up hours later to her mother calling out to her, "Winter... Suppertime."

Winter yelled out across the house, "Okay!"

Winter sat up and stretched as she yawned. She looked at Coby as she stood up.

"Time for supper, boy."

Coby jumped up out of bed and quickly followed behind her as she left the room and walked up the stairs to the kitchen where her father and mother sat at the table.

"Gary Towns chicken?" Winter asked as she sat at the table looking at the bucket of chicken in front of her.

"Yes, we were too tired from our camping trip to cook tonight so we just ordered Gary Towns."

Winter's mother replied as she poured herself a glass of soda. Winter nodded and scooped up some taters and placed them on her plate. Winter never complained. She was just happy her family was together eating supper at the table and not in front of the T.V. like some families. Winter finished up quickly and put her plate in the sink.

"I think I'm going to bed, six a.m. comes early,"

Winter stated as she excused herself from dinner, "Good night, my love." Winter's father got up and gave her a hug, "Love you, Winter. Sleep well."

Winter's mother gave her hug as well. They were a close family.

"Thanks, night, guys."

Winter headed down stairs to her bedroom alone. Coby was asleep by his food dish and she didn't want to wake him. Winter quickly got undressed and got into her P.Js. Winter's heart seemed to be beating out of her throat. She felt this way sometimes. Winter had a very bad anxiety disorder where she would get random attacks and think she was dying. They really scared her but after a while of having them she learned how to deal with them better.

She closed her eyes and took a few deep breaths. She laid there, thinking about what her doctor had said to her at her last appointment, *"When you have anxiety, you need to ground yourself. Bring you back to reality. Think of three things you can see, three things you can feel psychically and three things you can hear."*

Winter opened her eyes and started to say out loud what she could see. She looked around her room, "My computer, I see my stuffed giraffe I got on my last trip, I see pictures of my family on my mirror…"

Winter took another deep breath and started to feel around her. As she did, Coby pushed the room door open with his nose and jumped onto the bed. Winter smirked quickly, then started to concentrate again.

"I feel Coby licking my leg, ha, ha, ha, I feel my warm blanket on my bed, I feel my skin. I hear…"

Finally, Winter started to calm down and relax, "What a weekend." Winter whispered to Coby. Coby wiggled his way up to Winter's face and started to snuggling into her chest. Winter hugged him back and closed her eyes and smiled.

Shortly after, both, Coby and Winter, fell asleep.

Chapter 10
New Year – Old Heart

Winter was a busy young woman working five days a week as a receptionist in an accounting office. If she wasn't taking calls from clients or dealing with appointments and clients in person, she was running errands for her wicked boss. And when she wasn't do that, she was organizing client files and importing new information into them.

"Keep those filed up to date and make sure you lock up when you leave. Take the information port with you over the holidays and I will see you first thing on the second."

Winter stood up quickly grabbed her bosses fur jacket off the rack. While she helped her put her jacket on, all Winter could think about was how much she looked like that evil lady from 101 Dalmatians. Cruella, de-veil, I believe. Winter smirked and reached around her boss to open the door for her. "Don't worry, everything will be done just the way you like it and I will be here at eight a.m. sharp to tidy up and get everything ready for the new year."

Winter's boss lifted her chin up and left the office in a huff. Winter watched as her boss made her way over the icy path to her black Cadillac escalade with the chrome rims. Taylor quickly made her way to the window to watch her leave as well. As soon as Taylor poked her head through the blinds, their boss slipped and fell on the ice, both of them burst into laughter as they watched her struggling in her heels to get back up and into her high class S.U.V.

"We should have gone to help her... I know its mean...but..." Taylor cut Winter off. "But so, so funny!!!"

They both held their hands over their mouths as their boss waved from the vehicle as she left the parking lot. As soon as she was out of sight, the two of them laughed out loud again. "Omg, that was great!" Taylor laughed once more as she walked back to her desk. "I can't wait to get out of here and toke up. After this day, we had I'm glad we have until New Year's off." Taylor shut off her computer and cleaned up her work area as they chatted. "Same, well glad about the days off," Winter cleaned up her desk and quickly swept the building. Taylor grabbed her jacket, galaxy, looking jacket and her black satchel.

"Coming? Were gonna miss the bus," Taylor grabbed her bus pass out of her bag and went to the front door. Winter hurried and put the broom back in the storage closet and grab her things to go. Winter rechecked the list in her mind of things she needed to do before leaving the office. "Got that... that's done...yup... Yup..." Winter kept second guessing herself.

"Winnnerrr, lest go!" Taylor pulled on her furry winter boots as she yelled.

"Okay, Okay, I'm coming," Winter grabbed the keys out of her pocket and locked up the door. She pulled the handle to make sure it was locked. As she did, Taylor grabbed her arm, "Its locked! We have to go." She dragged Winter away from the door and they both scuffed their way quickly through the snow. Running across the street, through a parking lot and onto the side walk, just making it in time to catch the bus. "This is mine, I will see you soon, okay?" Taylor jumped onto the bus and the bus left as soon as she sat. Winter's bus was running late today due to an accident blocking her side of town. As Winter patently waited, another bus came to drop off its passengers. Winter played with her phone not noticing Mark getting off the bus and walking straight towards her. Winter felt someone standing behind her and jolted as the person placed their hand on her shoulder. "Hey, looking good." Winter turned around quickly pushing his hand off of her shoulder. "What do you want, Mark?" Winter asked in an irritated tone.

"Just on my way home from work like everyone else… Saw you standing there and you looked pretty cold so I thought I could come over and we could huddle up and chat." Mark placed his hand back on her shoulder as he did Winter pulled away. "I'm fine, thanks, that's what my jacket is for," Mark shook his head. "Winter, I just want to talk… Maybe we can grab a coffee?" Winter laughed and turned away.

"You are crazy, Mark. Leave me alone."

As she turned, her bus pulled into the lot.

"*Thank, God,*" she thought as she entered the bus a feeling of ease filled her body. She plopped herself into a seat as the other passengers got on board. Winter leaned back and closed her eyes. Mark entered the bus and walked to the back where Winter was sitting and sat next to her. Winter, nervous, now shifted as close to the window as she could.

"I'm not going to hurt you babe, I miss you."

“This isn’t your bus, Mark,” Winter said with anger in her voice. Making believe she was brave when she was clearly not. She shook as he spoke.

“I can just take the connecting one at the next stop, no big deal, just wanted to tell you I care about you and I miss us,” Mark smiled as the bus pulled up to the next stop. “I’ll see you around, Lucky.” Mark swung around the bus pole and made his way off the bus and onto the street. Winter’s heart pounded in her chest as she repeated his words over and over in her head.

“I’ll see you around… Lucky.”

Winter shook with disgusted shivers as the bus closed the doors and left to continue its route.

Winter got home in about 30 minutes, which was great, considering the accident on the road was still getting cleaned up. It looked like it was a bad one, but no one was hurt luckily. Winter walked inside the house and shook off her jacket.

“I’m home,” Winter shouted out as her mother peeked around the kitchen arch way.

“Off for the holidays now, sweetie?”

Winter nodded, “Yup, I sure am.”

Winter looked around the room, “Where’s dad?”

“Oh. Shoot, I forgot to tell you your friend, Justin, came over to see you but you were late coming home so him and dad are in the garage hanging out.”

Winter’s mom started cutting the potatoes for supper as Winter’s jaw dropped.

“Justin is here?”

“Yes, in the garage. Your father already likes him better than Mark.”

Winter shook her head in disbelief. "Justin…is here?"

"Yeah, he's having trouble with his truck and your father wanted to take a look for him."

Winter's head started spinning as she tried to figure out what in the world to do. She slowly made her way to the garage door and slowly opened it peering out from the crack.

"Haha, right on, my son. Proper thing." Winter's father laughed as Justin pointed to the window of his rusty dodge. "Well, that's where the window was supposed to be but the tree wanted to let me have some air conditioning, I guess."

Both of them laughed. Winter squinted her eyes at them through the crack, "You got to be kidding me." Winter opened the door all the way now, no more hiding. "Justin…what are you doing here?" Justin quickly walked over towards her. "Ahhh, came over to see you but your bus was late. I was going to come grab you but my truck shits the bed in your driveway." Winter looked at her dad and raised her eyebrows, hoping he would somehow read her mind and make Justin leave. But that's not what happened.

"You can borrow my car, buddy, until we can get your truck going again."

Winter's eyes felt like they were going to pop out of her sockets as she heard her father. She glared over at him as he gave Justin the keys, "All I ask is when you bring her back, fill her up for me." Justin graciously thanked Winter's father as he took the keys from his hands.

"Your dad is awesome, Winter."

Winter rolled her eyes, "Yes, I know, he's *my* dad." Winter sighed and went back inside, "I got to do some things, I'll see you later Justin."

"Yes, you will!" Justin smiled at Winter as she walked away. Winter's father nudged Justin, "Now, she's still my daughter, buddy." Justin laughed and thanked him again for the car and left. Winter's dad made his way into the house, as he did, Winter confronted him, "Why did you do that?" Winter folded her arms as she stood on top of the staircase looking down at her father.

"Do what? Loan you friend the car?"

"Mmmhmm."

Winter started tapping her foot like a mother, waiting for their miscreant daughter to get home from a party that she sunk out to.

"I was just helping out a buddy."

Winter groaned in frustration, "Uggggggghhh!"

Winter stomped her way down the stairs and into her room. She was done with this day. So done with it. She covered herself up with the blanket on her bed and hide under the sheets. And that's where she stayed for the rest of the night.

Winter had seen Justin off and on all her holiday break. It was sad to say but she just wanted to go back to work. Anywhere would have been better then feeling uncomfortable in her own home. Christmas was over and it was finally New Year's Eve. Only two days until work. Justin finally got his truck working again and hadn't been over for two days, which was a nice break for Winter. Tonight, I am not going anywhere, I'm going to stay at home play board games with my mom while Dad is at work and just relax. Winter and her mother loved playing games together. They played Skip-Bo, Uno, and Sorry. Drank wine and had snacks. It was a perfectly relaxing night. Well 12 O' clock came around they both hugged each other.

"Well, time for bed for me."

Winter's mother got up from the table and brought the games back into the game closet.

"Yeah, I'm going to go play a few video games before I hit the hay," Winter said as her mother closed the closet and made her way to her room. "Okay, love, try to get some sleep."

Winter's mother closed the door behind her. Winter turned on her gaming system and loaded one of her favorite games. Just as she did her phone began to rang. Thinking it was a friend, wishing her happy new year, she quickly picked up. "Happy New Year!" Winter exclaimed as she answered the call.

"Winter…" a voice slurred over the phone. "I need your help…"

Winter looked at the caller I.D. since the voice wasn't recognizable, "Mark, what the hell are you doing calling me at this hour? Actually, what are you doing calling me at all?"

Winter was just about to hang up when Mark seemed like he was…crying?

"What's wrong, Mark?" Winter softly spoke as she pressed her ear to the phone so she could hear him. "I'm drunk, I spent all my money so I can't get a cab and I'm walking home. I'm close by your house now…but. But I don't think I'll make it home al…one…lone…by myself. I think I'll freeze in a snow bank before…I… gets home." Mark slurred every few words. Winter had a hard time hearing him but she understood.

"Mark, I don't think…"

Mark cut her off mid refusal, "Please, Wiinterrr. Just walk me home and never see me again."

Winter sighed and agreed to help him. Winter had been drinking also so she wasn't driving anywhere. Winter grabbed her jacket and quickly made her way out to the main roadway where she found Mark stumbling down the side walk.

"Oh, what a mess you're in Mark."

As Mark gotten closer, he stumbled over his own feet and into Winter's arms. She struggled to keep him up off the ground. "Come on, Mark, work with me here." Mark quickly stood up and grabbed her arm, "I'm… I'm so glad, so happy you came." Winter pushed him up off her and wrapped his arm around her, so she could try and balance him. "Yeah this is the last thing I'm doing for you." Winter and Mark walked through the falling snow in -30C. It was a very chilly night. Winter just wanted to drop him off and get home in bed. Half way there, Mark stopped by the side benches, "I need to stop." Mark sat on the ice- and snow-covered bench and tucked his head down in his jacket and started to mumble. "Mark, come on, we can't stop were almost there." Winter shivered as she tried to yank mark up off the bench. Mark pushed her away, "Mark, I don't have time for this, okay? Come on…"

Mark quickly stood up in rage.

"My father left me at a young age, and now you, the only person I loved left me, too?"

He turned around and kicked the bench. "Mark, stop, I'm here… I didn't leave, I'm here…"

Winter trying everything to calm him down.

"You didn't even *love me, did you*?" Mark swung his arms around as he yelled out his feelings and thoughts.

"Mark, of course, I did stop it, you're going to wake the people living in the houses behind us."

Winter slowly reached her arm out to place it on his back to calm him down. As she did, he grabbed her arm and with his steel toe boots kicked her as hard as he could. He slammed his fist onto the back of her head, knocking her down into the snow. Winter started to cry. She yelled, "What the heck are you doing, Mark? I'm trying to help you! You hurt me!"

Winter pushed herself up off the cold ground and turned to walk back home, "You have issues you need to get help, Mark." Winter started to walk away as she did Mark fell into the snow onto his back.

"I should just stay here and freeze to death, anyways, I should die… What's the point?"

Mark laid there in the snow bank. As he did, Winter contemplated leaving him there but couldn't. "Fuck, Mark, why am I so nice?" Winter hurried her way back to him and pulled him up out of the snow bank and brushed him off with her hands. She wrapped his arms around her shoulders once more and grabbed onto his belt to keep him up. After a long stumbling ten-minute walk, they reached the front door of Mark's house.

"Here, now go to bed. I'm out of here."

Winter opened the door and helped him inside as she let go he fell to his knees. Winter sighed, "Ugh, Fine." She took off her boots and grabbed his arm, helping him down over the stairs to his bed room. He stumbled back and forth until he finally made it to his bed. He fell back onto his back and closed his eyes. "You good?" Winter asked as she grabbed her phone from her pocket.

"Yes, come sleep with me." Mark drunkenly waved his arm, trying to guide her towards him.

"Nah, I'm going home now."

Winter called her mother as she picked up Mark quickly jumped out of bed and twisted her arm behind her back.

"Winter? Its two a.m., are you okay?"

Mark tightened his grip on her arm and whispered in her ear, tell your mother you are okay and you're staying here with me. Winter struggled but couldn't get away from his grasp. "You don't want to make me mad."

Mark twisted her arm a little more.

"I'm fine, sorry, Mom, I was going to get you to come get me but I decided to stay at Marks for the night." Winter's mother seemed very concerned on the phone.

"You wanted to come home and you changed your mind that quick? I'll come get you."

Winter started to panic as Marks grip became even more tight it was hurting so bad now, Winter knew if he twisted much more it would break. "No, no. I'm good, Mom, I'll see you tomorrow morning, love you."

"Winter, I'm going to call your fath—"

Mark grabbed the phone and turned it off. He let go of her arm and threw her phone on the chair. Mark picked Winter up and threw her onto his bed against the wall. He laid next to her and cuddled into her. He slides off her pants and tore off her underwear. He stuck his cock inside her took a few pumps and finished, "Ahhh, that's good." Mark held her so tight she could barely breath if she moved. She was trapped, and scared. She just wanted to go home. But that wasn't happening right now. He quickly fell asleep still tightly grasped to Winter's body. Winter wiggled but couldn't get free. Winter softly sobbed for hours as the pain from the abuse finally hit her. She was a strong girl but this is the moment, she finally was broken. A few hours in the same position, Mark turned to his other side, finally letting her go. She quickly and quietly slid off the bed and grabbed her pants. She slid them on, grabbed her phone, and ran. She ran up the stairs, and out the door. She ran down the street and up the road as fast as she could go. She hasn't run like this is a long, long time, not since volleyball in high school during training. It took her a short time to get home. She slowed down when her house was in her sight. The sun was slowly coming up and the air was still freezing cold. Her face burned as she stopped to catch her breath. Winter took a few deep breaths and walked into her house, trying to be quiet she slowly pushed the door open. As she did, her mother sat on the stairs waiting for her.

"Mom, why are you awake? Its only six a.m.!"

Winter softly closed the door behind her and kicked off her boots.

"I was worried, wanted to make sure you were okay."

Winter's mother stood up and helped winter take off her jacket. As she did, she noticed bruises all over her arms.

"Did he do this to you?"

Winter quickly grabbed her jacket from her mothers' hands and hung it up in the closet. Winter was speechless.

"If you go back to him you, deserve what he's doing to you. Your smarter than this."

Winter nodded and made her way back down into her bedroom. She pushed the door shut and cuddled into Coby who was asleep on her bed. Winter cried…and cried…and cried until she fell asleep. Tears rolled down her face and stained her blouse, she lay there, beautifully broken. A New Year, an old heart.

Chapter 11
Get out There

It was now the end of February and Winter was working hard at the office. Taylor rolled her chair out from her desk, down the hall and into Winter's desk, right next to her.

"Can I help you?" Winter joked as she watched Taylor comically roll herself to her like a child playing with a spinney chair for the first time.

"You should get yourself out there again. You've been so sad lately and I think you need to go out on a date."

Taylor started pulling Winter's chair and rolling her away from her computer desk.

"Taylor, I have to get these files sent out today, I'm busy."

Taylor pushed Winter back to her desk. Winter turned her chair to face Taylor.

"Plus, I'm not ready for a relationship yet."

Taylor laughed, "I never said you have to marry the guy, I just think you could get a free meal and a nice time out of it."

Winter shook her head.

"Just think about it okay?" Taylor threw a paper airplane to Winter with a website on it, "It's a good dating site, my friends use it."

Winter looked down at the paper and balled it up and stuffed it in her bag.

"Thanks…" Winter said, trying to get Taylor off her back.

"I just want you to be happy, Winner, again, okay?"

Winter pondered in what Taylor had said.

Am I depressed? Maybe I should go on a date? What's the harm in a date? Winter thought about it all night and decided to sign up for this dating site anyways. Winter scrolled down, filled out her profile, and submitted it.

"Oh, this is cringy."

Winter shook her head and closed the app. Moments later, she had three messages from three different guys.

"Wow…okay."

First message, *"Wanna fuck?"*

"Ugh, really?"

Next… Winter opened the next one.

"Hi, my name is Dustin, I'm 28 years old, I love rap and just chilling with my dog, Dexter, and of course, getting a good-looking gal on my dick. Give me a message back if you want to chicken noodle with me."

Winter shook her head and held in a laugh as she read, "It was okay until that part."

Winter wasn't catholic but she made the shape of the cross over her body by moving her hand from the head to the chest and then from shoulder to shoulder.

"Here, we go,"

Winter opened the last message.

"Hey, I'm Richard, I read your profile and you seemed pretty cool. Looking hot, too, I'm free tonight would you like to go out for dinner and a movie? Here's my number, text me and I'll come get you."

Winter's face blushed as she couldn't believe she got a response to easily. She quickly texted the number and made arrangements for the date. She had 30 minutes to get ready before the date. When she slid on her second shoe, she heard a honk from outside. It was Richard. He wasn't super attractive but he seemed to have his shit together from his profile so that's all that mattered. She opened the car door and buckled up.

"Hey, I'm Winter."

Richard smiled and introduced himself too. He seemed like a real ladies' man. Dinner was great he paid even though winter insisted. This night was going great. They chatted about work, about family, and about weed.

"So, you smoke?" Richard asked as they drove.

"Not often, just when I'm with my friend, Taylor, trying to relax."

Richard nodded.

"Cool, hey would you like to come to my place and watch a movie?"

Winter agreed and they made their way to his apartment. It was a small, older apartment but had a rustic charm to it. Richard parked his car and went on inside. Winter, a little thrown off, quickly followed behind. They sat on the couch in the tiny living room. He flicked through the movies on the television.

"So, what would you like to watch? A scary movie? Comedy?"

Winter thought, "Hmmm… Comedy is always a great option."

Richard agreed. All of a sudden, his two roommates got home and they were loud and defiantly drunk. "We're not going to be able to watch a movie in here," Richard stood up off the couch and point to the room over the stairs. "That's my room, you go up there and we will watch the movie there instead."

Richard smiled and Winter followed his commands like a puppy. Winter walked into the room and sat at the end of the bed. As she did, she scanned the room for a T.V. But there was no T.V. in sight. As soon as she realized, the door shut and locked.

"Don't worry, hun, lay back. I forgot my T.V. is broken."

Winter started to get an uneasy feeling in her stomach. "Maybe we can just go for a drive," Winter suggestion was ignored. Richard pulled his pants down and opened a condom he had on his night stand. He slid it over her, cock and sat next to winter. "I don't want to do this," Winter said in a nervous tone.

"It's okay it's no big deal, just lay back, I'll do it, you don't have to."

He pushed winter's body gently back onto his bed and started to pull her panties off slowly. He forced his cock inside her and with three thrusts, he was finished and quickly got up and left the room. Winter covered herself up in the blanket and sunk into the sheets. Richard entered the room with just his boxers on. You can stay the night; I'll give you a ride home in the morning. He got in bed and fell asleep cuddling into Winter like she was some sort of Teddy bear. Winter laid, there looking up at the ceiling fan as it spun.

"Was I just raped? No, I wasn't raped, but I said no, but I did lay back, but he did push me, but…" thoughts crashed back and forth in her head as she drifted off to sleep.

7:30 a.m., Winter's alarm went off, both Richard and Winter jumped.

"Oh shit, Work!" Winter jumped up and ran to the bathroom. "I'll get dressed and drop you off," Winter quickly grabbed her purse and grabbed her hair brush. She did her makeup quickly and got into the car. Richard was waiting outside. Winter's job wasn't too far away from Richards building which was a bonus for her today. Richard pulled up outside the building.

"Here ya go. We will talk later."

Winter waved as she ran to the door. She unlocked the door and quickly got inside. As she did, Taylor scuffed her way up the path and in through the door.

"Man, its cold out there," Taylor shook off her boots and unzipped her jacket. Winter walked over to the coffee maker and made herself a tea.

"You're wearing a dress in 20°C? Are you crazy?"

Winter blushed.

"I was on a date last night and he just dropped me off."

Taylor hopped in excitement, "You dirty dog! You stayed the night!"

Taylor skipped around the room.

"It wasn't like that…" Winter softly replied as Taylor kept shouting out across the office, "Winter got laid, Winter got laid!" Winter pulled Taylor aside as the wicked witch entered the office space. The room went quiet.

"Winter, turn on my opera please. Disk 1, track 2. And don't forget my coffee, I've already had a rough morning!"

"I'm on it, boss."

Winter dragged Taylor with her as they whispered, "Let's just not talk about it okay? It didn't go great."

Taylor nodded.

"Okay, my lips, are sealed."

Taylor went back to her desk as Winter turned on the Opera and made the witches brew.

The day went long as not many clients were needing much assistance with taxes in February. As Winter was finishing up, her work her cell began to vibrate on the desk. Winter quickly picked the phone up off her desk and read the message that popped up on the screen.

"Richard"

"Hey, you were a terrible lay, so don't text me back again okay. We're done."

Winter deleted the text and placed the phone back on her desk. She quickly got up and went into the office washroom. She locked the door behind her and leaned against the door and took a deep breath. Winter's head began to feel faint but she kept calm. Winter stared into the mirror and watched tears fall from her eyes. Winter grabbed a tissue from the box on back of the staff toilet. She blew her nose and took another breath. Her heart felt empty and her mind weak. She didn't even want to have sex with that guy. But he didn't rape her, did he? She pulled herself together and fixed her mascara. Winter walked out of the bathroom looking like she didn't have a care in the world. She had a smile on her face but pain in her eyes. Winter was broken inside.

Months went by of the same routine. Work, eat, sleep, Work, eat, sleep. Finally, the day was here, May 8th. Winter was packing for her flight.

"Did you pack your toothbrush?"

Winter rolled her eyes as her mother shouted across the house.

"Mom, I'm 22 years old, of course, I packed my toothbrush."

Winter quickly ran to the bathroom and double checked to make sure she had actually packed her toothbrush, which she did not. She blushed as she grabbed her toothbrush from the holder and tip toed back to her room to place it in her suitcase.

Winter was dancing as she packed, her hips swayed back and forth to the beat in her head. A song she heard on the radio a few days ago that just didn't want to leave thoughts. Winter was extremely excited to fly and see her best friend, Aaron. They both were extremely excited. Winter hadn't been back home in ages. She uses to live close to Aaron but her parents moved when she was only 14. Winter was originally from a small island in Canada. It was beautiful there; the island was surrounded by sea. There were many trees and lots of wildlife. Most people were kind and had amazing hospitality, the dialect was a little strange to those who haven't heard it before and maybe a little hard to understand but winter missed it and was thrilled to be able to use it again. Winter zipped up her suitcase and dragged it off the bed and onto the floor. She pushed in on the little black button on her suitcase and pulled the handle up so she could wheel it down the hall. When she reached the steps, she pushed it back down and carried it one step at a time up to the front door. Winter's father was waiting outside the front door with a smoke in one hand and the keys in the other. "Ready, baby?" Winter's dad placed his smoke into his mouth, so his hand would be free to take his daughters luggage. Winter smiled as she handed over the heavy bag. Winter's father was taken back

"How long you going for? A year?" Winter's dad laughed as he carried the bag to the jeep. Winter shook her head at her father as she watched him try to squeeze it into the back seat. "I'm going to have to get a bigger vehicle."

Winter's father joked as he closed the back door.

"Dad, it isn't that bad!" Winter said in a fun poking way. Winter's father shook his head and smiled as he opened the door to get in the vehicle.

"No, my baby, Dad's just kidding around."

Winter's father sat inside and turned on the engine. Winter opened the passenger side door and pulled herself up into her seat. They both closed their doors, buckled up, and went on their way to the airport. The airport was about a 20-minute drive away from the house, and with Winter's father driving like he always did, it was really only about eight minutes and 49 seconds away.

"Dad!" Winter shouted as they slide around the turns. Winter's father laughed as he swayed back and forth down the road. "I'm just playing around; I would never hurt you."

Winter's face was covered in fear, "Yeah. I, I know."

Winter's father smiled at his daughter once more and pressed lightly on the breaks to slow down a little. "You know I can't do this with your mother in the vehicle."

Winter replied, "Oh, I know! Mom would kill ya!"

Winter laughed as her father took her fear and placed it on his face.

“Sometimes, I really think she wants to.”

They both let out an uncomfortable laugh as they pulled up to the terminal. Winter’s father parked as close to the door as he could and quickly hopped out of the jeep to grab her bag out of the back seat.

“So, how’s picking you up at the airport?” Winter’s dad handed her, her bag as he asked.

“Umm. Aunt Shelia and Uncle Lon. They are bringing me into town and dropping me off at Aaron’s place.” Winter’s father leaned in for a hug. He held her tightly and pulled her in close, “Be safe, okay?”

Winter smiled, “I’ll be fine, I love you.”

Winter fixed her handle on her bag and started to walk inside the airport, “I love you, too, baby girl.”

Winter’s father stood there until he couldn’t see her anymore.

Winter was one step closer to seeing her best friend. She really missed him the past couple months with all the crazy stuff that had been happening to her, she just needed an Aaron hug.

Chapter 12
Utopia

After a long 14 hours of switching planes and waiting in crowed terminals, Winter was on her last wing of her trip to the island. The intercom cut in and everyone on the plane became silent as the flight attendant spoke, "*Ladies and gentlemen, as we start our descent, please make sure your seats and tray tables are in their full upright position and stowed away. As you may have noticed, the seat belt sign in back on, so, please, make sure your seat belt is securely fastened and all carry-on luggage is stowed underneath the seat in front of you or in the overhead bins. Thank you.*"

Winter leaned over the sleeping man snoring next to her to try and look out the planes window. It was pretty early now, especially with the three-hour time difference. Winter's eyes sparkled as she peered out of the window. The sun shined bright as they left the clouds and became closer to the land. Winter's face became flushed with an intense feeling of love as she noticed her uncles and aunt's car in the airport parking lot. The plane quickly touched ground after that jolting awake the man sleeping next to her. Winter covered her mouth with her sweater, trying not to let the man see her smirk or hear her giggle. Another announcement came onto the intercom as the plane landed onto the runway, "*Please, keep your seat belts fastened until we come to a full stop and the seat belt sign is off. Thank you for flying with us today and we hope you have a great stay or visit on the island.*"

Winter squirmed in her seat as she stared down the seat belt sign until the light went out. Winter quickly unbuckled herself and jumped out of her seat. She stood on her tip toes and tugged her bag out of the overhead bin above her seat. Winter shook with excitement as the people in the plane started to walk forward in the narrow isle. The excitement must have been visible on her face because the man in front of her smiled and asked, "You must be visiting family from away, because you are just glowing." The man smiled at winter. He was an elder man, maybe about 70 years old or more. His hair was curly, short, and pure white. He was wearing a yellow scarf with a long brown jacket. Holding a cane in one hand and a little black bag in the other. His voice was a little cracked but so very sweet. He looked like how I would picture Santa Clause if he were a real person.

"If you didn't know that already…ummm. I was just kidding, of course he is a real person."

Cough.

Anyways… Winter's cheeks rose up to her eyes as she responded to the cute little old man.

"Yeah, haven't been here for a while. Visiting friends and family for a week or so," the man smiled and then a wave of sadness quickly turned his face. "I was just visiting my daughter and grandchildren, they moved away for work so I don't get to see them very often. And as I get older, it is becoming harder to fly."

The man buttoned his jacket up and fixed his scarf as they slowly moved forward towards the exit.

"I'm sorry, I know it's hard when you're so far away from love ones. But I bet you made a lot of amazing memories when you went to visit."

The man smiled and pulled out a small wallet sized picture from his bag, "Yes, we did. There is my grandson, Marshall, and my granddaughter, Lyrica."

He pointed at the picture as Winter bent over to take a closer look.

"Very adorable kids."

Winter smiled and lightly touched the man's back. The man looked up at Winter and carefully placed the photo back into his bag. As he did, it was their turn to exit the plane.

"You have yourselves a wonderful day," the stewardess kindly said as they exited the plane and entered the tunnel connected to the airport from the plane's door. Both, Winter and the man, nodded as they walked forward.

"It was very nice meeting you, darlin'," the sweet old man said as he hobbled his way up the ramp. "I'm Bryan, by the way."

Winter responded, "It was great meeting you, too, hun, I'm Winter." The man waved at her as they went their separate ways. As Winter walked through the airport, she spotted her tall and skinny uncle and her short and adorable aunt standing by the door with a trolley. As Winter saw them, she quickened her steps towards them. "How was your flight?" Winter's aunt, Shelia, gave her a big hug. "Good, good thanks."

As Shelia hugged her niece, Lonny softly spoke, "Well, let's go, I don't feel safe being this close to bishop falls."

Winter and Aunt Shelia both laughed and started to walk out to the car. Bishop falls was a place Winter's aunt liked to go to visit her sister. And usually, when she went there, Winter's uncle was home alone with no one to cook for him, he didn't like that much. He would joke about it a lot but he was really the sweetest man you would ever meet. He was a lot like Winter's pop that way.

Unfortunately, he died from A.L.S. a few years later. If you haven't heard about A.L.S. before, you should definitely look it up and donate. It's a very worthy cause, but that's another sad story that Winter doesn't experience yet, so let's continue.

Lon grabbed the bag and threw it into the trunk of the grey Toyota corolla. Winter and Shelia both already in the car, Lon slowly ducked into the car and put it in reverse to back out of the spot.

"So, are you going to stay with us again?" Shelia asked.

Winter always stayed with them while she was visiting the island. Winter even lived with them for a while back in high school. Lonny smirked like he was about to say something funny and quietly listened as he drove. Winter looked up at her uncle.

"I see that sweet, evil look on your face, Uncle Lon!"

Everyone laughed and Winter replied, "I may stay a night or two if that's okay, but I'll be spending most of my time at my friend Aaron's house."

Shelia nodded and Lonny spoke softly, "Thank goodness for that, I'll be able to sleep without listening to the loud tapping of your computer keyboard."

He laughed quietly.

"Hey, I was a teenager, of course, I was going to be loud! I know you love me!"

Shelia looked over at her husband as he blushed.

"You are just like your aunts, all trouble makers besides Glenda."

We all laughed once more as uncle finished joshing with her.

"Speaking of Glenda, she came out from Deer Lake to come visit you."

Winter lightening up with excitement, "Auntie Glenda is here?"

Winter did a silly dance in the back seat as she heard the news. Winter loved all her aunts but her and Auntie Glenda had a special bond. 35 minutes later, they pulled up the long gravel driveway to the big, yellow house on the hill, facing the ocean. Winter got out of the car and grabbed her bag from the trunk. She leaned back so she should see around the trees to look at her old family home. Winter's heart melted. She was finally home.

"Come on, it's too hot to be outside today."

Winter's uncle, Lonny, closed the door, leaving it open a crack. Winter ran and rushed inside, closing the door behind her. She quickly kicked off her shoes and walked right into their spare room where she always stayed when she visited. She placed her bag on the end of the mattress. As she did, she noticed Auntie Glenda's pajamas laying out on top of the bed. A huge smile came onto Winter's face. As she turned to walk out of the room, Auntie Glenda walked in. "How's aunties girl?" Winter ran and squeezed her aunt tightly. "I missed you so, so much!"

Winter let go and stood there looking at her auntie. Auntie Glenda was a very short woman. She had short, greyish, blonde hair and cute little oval shaped glasses. She usually wore jeans with a cute T-shirt, usually something pastel colored. Her smile would light up a room when she walked in. Glenda turned and walked out into the hall way.

"Come on my, baby, Aunt Glenda made you some bread pudding."

Winter scampered down the hall behind her auntie like a little girl trying not to lose her mother in a large shopping center. When they reached the kitchen, Winter's uncle was already sitting at the head of the table with a cup of tea and a few biscuits on a small plate.

"Sit down and eat your dinner now," Lon softly said, pointing to the chair next to him.

"Aren't you going to eat, Uncle?" Winter questioned as she sat on the wooden chair beside him. He smirked and shook his head, "I ate at dinner time."

He pointed at the clock on the wall. It read 1:04 p.m. Winter rolled her eyes in a playful way and responded. "Oh, of course, I'm sorry," she said in a sarcastic voice. Lon smiled and everyone smirked at him. Lonny liked to have a set time for his meals. Meal time was meal time and that was that.

"Now I know some of you are like wait… Isn't dinner time like six p.m.? Well, it is in most places but on the island, we call lunch time, around 12 p.m. dinner time and dinner time, supper. It isn't too big of a difference and it might sound silly but that's just the way it is there."

"Here you are, my lover," Glenda placed a plate down in front of Winter at the table. It was potatoes, carrots, turnip, chicken, bread pudding (an onion bread), and gravy all spread out. On the island, we call it jigs dinner.

"Eat up, my lover."

Winter's taste buds were thrilled when the bread pudding touched her mouth. Winter closed her eyes and enjoyed her first bite of her auntie's famous pudding.

"Yummy...so delicious, Auntie Glenda, thank you."

Glenda leaned over and kissed Winter's cheek, "You know Aunt Glenda wouldn't let you come here without some bread pudding."

Winter smiled and continued stuffing her face with the feast presented in front of her. After dinner, they chatted for the rest of the day, and when the sun went down, the card games came out. Winter, Glenda, and Shelia played games all night until one a.m.

"I think it's time for me to hit the hay."

Winter stood up from the table and brought her empty glass of water to the sink.

"Yes, I suppose it is."

They all cleaned up and went to their rooms for a good night's rest. Winter was in heaven. She loved her family and missed them very much. She was so happy to be back on the island. Winter went into her room and closed the door. Everything was exactly the same from where she stayed there as a teen. She pulled out her phone from her pocket and texted Aaron.

"Hey, I'm here, I'll see you tomorrow."

Aaron responded back right away.

"I'm so excited! I can't wait!" Winter smiled and curled up into the bed. Her aunt and uncles had a very familiar smell. It reminded Winter of her childhood. She felt safe,

warm, and happy there. She hadn't felt those emotions in along long time.

Morning came and Winter woke up to the smell of bacon and eggs. Winter wasn't a huge fan of breakfast foods but something about the island made her really enjoy the simple things in life, including breakfast. "Morning, angel face, sleep good?" Aunt Glenda mixed her tea as walked towards the table.

"Where's Uncle Lon and Aunt Shelia?"

Uncle is gone to church to help the pastor with some renovations and Aunt Shelia is gone to bishop falls for the day. Winter scuffed her way to the table, dragging a loose blanket with her. She sat at the table in front of a large plate of food. There were eggs, bacon, fresh homemade bread with homemade strawberry jam, and tones of different juices to choose from.

"Auntie, you didn't need to make all this food, it's just the two of us," Winter giggled in amazement as she scanned the table for a fork.

"Only the best for Aunt Glenda's girl."

Winter rested her arm on the table and her head on her hand.

"Oh Auntie, I love you."

Glenda quickly responded, "I love you, too, now eat your breakfast."

They both ate and cleaned up together. Auntie washed and Winter dried. They both packed away the dishes and headed to their rooms to get dressed for the day. Winter opened her suit case and pulled out a black top with a pair of thin, camo leggings. *It was a warm day on the island but never too warm for black*, she thought. As she pulled her tank top over herself, her cell phone vibrated right off the dresser. “Oh, shit,” Winter said in an irritated voice. She picked up and answered the phone.

“Hello?”

“Winter! I’m coming to get you now, are you at your aunt and uncles or your uncle Boyd’s?”

Winter spoke fast, “I’m at my uncle and auntie’s house, the yellow one on top of the hill by my old place. You know the one I’m taking about, it used to be the only yellow one until the family down the road changed their siding and now they have a yellow house, too, but theirs is at the bottom of the hill and I’m at the one on the top of the hill.” Winter took a breath.

“Yeah, okay, girl, calm your nerves, I’ll be there in a few. Love ya!” Aaron hung up and winter rushed to gather her things. She was so eager to get over to Aaron’s and just chill like old times.

Winter kissed her auntie good bye and dragged her suit case outside onto the deck as she looked over the hill waiting for Aaron to show up. Within just a few moments, Aaron drove up the gravel driveway in his little, blue Volkswagen buggy. Aaron quickly put his car in park half way up the driveway and swung open the door and started to run the rest of the way up.

“Winter!”

Aaron and Winter collided as they both ran to each other. It kind of looked like a cheesy scene from a romantic movie where everything slows down as the couple runs towards each other, panning back and forth until they embrace for a moment and then the man lifts the girl up and spins her around. Well, it did, until they literally bonked heads and fell to the ground almost breaking each other on the way down. They laid on the ground laughing and hugging. "It seems like forever since I have seen you!" Aaron hugged her tighter as they rolled around on the rocks. "I'm so happy right now."

Winter started to cry happy tears.

Aaron stood up and reached his hand down to help Winter up off the ground, "Come on, bitch, let's go catch up at my place." Winter grabbed his hand and hopped up of the ground brushing her butt off as she walked around to the car's passenger door. Aaron bolted across the driveway and grabbed Winter's bag for her.

"Forgot something, you silly bitch?'" Aaron laughed as he carried the bag to his baby blue bug.

"Shit, I almost forgot it."

Aaron sat in the driver seat, put his sunglasses on, and buckled up. He turned his head toward Winter before reversing down the drive way. With his glasses down a little on his nose, he replied with a sassy voice, "What would you do without me?"

Winter shook her head and grinned as Aaron back down the driveway onto the street.

"Hold on, here we go!"

Aaron slammed on the gas and they jolting forward, speeding down the empty street. The windows were down and Winter hair flew all over the place with the wind. The smell of salt water filled the car as they drove.

"It's so nice to be home again. I really miss the ocean."

Winter took a deep breath in enjoying the fresh air. Aaron pushed his sunglasses up and started to interrogate Winter.

"So that asshole, Mark… He's out of your life for good now?"

Winter nodded.

"He was a terrible guy, Winter."

Winter looked out the window, "Let me catch you up on a few things." Winter started talking about Mark, Justin, and Richard as they got closer to their destination. Aaron teared up as he drove just listening to Winter's stories.

"Garrell, we got to stop down here for a quick second."

Winter, a bit confused, tilted her head as they pulled into a closed in driveway with a ghetto looking house at the end of it.

"What are we doing here? This is freaky."

Winter shifted down in her seat as Aaron unbuckled.

"After all the shit you've been through and the 'tea' you just spilt on me, we need some Mary Jane."

Aaron closed the door and walked up to the dark creepy house. It was an old house, it looked as if it were in a house fire but never got renovated after. The siding was half melted and the rest was barely hanging on the house. The yard was covered in random vehicle parts and the deck on the side of the house was full of random people drinking and smoking.

Aaron walked around the yard and over to the deck where everyone was. After a good ten-minute wait, a huge dude with tattoos all over his body and longer hair than most of the woman at the house appeared. Aaron stuffed a baggy in his pant pocket and strolled back to the vehicle. Aaron got back into his car and buckled up once again.

"Let's get home and smoke this shit."

Winter chuckled as they went back onto the road.

They arrived at Aaron house. The house was a small cottage looking home. The outside was like from a fairytale. The walk way to the wooden door was simple yet charming. There were flowers all along the sides of the walkway. There were vines hanging off the roof and around the windows of the house. It almost looked like Snow White lived here.

"Ummm, WTF, Aaron, when did you move into a Disney film?"

Aaron smirked as he pulled out his keys and unlocked the door.

"This place was cheap so I grabbed it. I won the hairdressing competition so I used the prize money to put towards this place."

Winter was stunned when she walked inside the cute little cottage. Everything was so much bigger than it looked from the outside. Her eyes wandered around the room as she started to take off her shoes.

"Here, let me put your bag in our room," Aaron snatched the bag from Winter's hands and marched straight into the bedroom. Winter slowly followed behind, looking around as she followed him.

"What a beautiful little house, Aaron."

Aaron dropped her bag onto the bench at the end of the bed and replied, "It's perfect for me, just a one bedroom, one-bathroom, small kitchen, and a tiny living space."

Aaron flicked on the T.V. and started to shimmy the weed out of his pant pocket. Winter flopped down on the couch beside him, pull papers out of the tiny box that was on the coffee table in front of them. Aaron leaned down and put his hand under the couch. He slid a silver tray out from under it and placed it on top of the table. He grinded the weed and made two of the most perfect joints winter has ever seen. "I still can't make a decent joint," Winter said as she watched Aaron roll his heart out.

"All in the wrist, honey," Aaron joked as he passed her a lighter and her own joint. "This stuff is all T.H.C. I've never had it before. It's a new strain he just got in."

Aaron smelt his joint before putting it into his mouth to light up. Winter did the same and they both lit their joints and took a deep puff. Both of them sunk into the couch as they continued to enjoy their blunts. Moments later, Aaron and Winter both looked at each other as their stomachs grumbled. Aaron pointed to his stomach as he slurred his words, "This bitch needs some snacks." Aaron stood up from the couch and walked into the bathroom looking at himself in the mirror. Winter, in a dazed state, walked over to the bathroom as well and hugged into Aaron as he fixed his hair.

"Let's go get snacks," Winter giggled as they both decided to walk to the store down the street. Half way there, Aaron started to crack up laughing randomly. Winter turned to him and started to laugh, too, after a good minute of laughing, Winter stopped Aaron and asked. "Why are we laughing?" Aaron kept laughing and then pushed Winter into a bush in some random person's yard. Aaron fell to his knees laughing so hard he could hardly breathe, "I'm going to piss my pants, Winter."

Winter kicked her legs, "Aaron… Aaron, I'm stuck."

Aaron continued to laugh as Winter struggled to get up. They both laughed so hard. "You look like a bush person!"

Aaron continued as he attempted to rescue Winter from the bush.

They finally got their snacks and went back to Aaron's place. The walk back was very uneventful and it didn't take long before both of them passed out on the couch while watching a random cartoon on T.V. They both looked so peaceful as they slept. Cuddling into each other with smiles on their faces. They both missed each other and felt almost complete together.

The next morning, Aaron woke up before Winter. He carefully lifted Winter's arm off of him and quietly got up and went to the bathroom. When the bathroom door shut and the shower turned on, Winter slowly fluttered her eyes open and closed. She yawned a big yawn and stretched her arms above her head and arched her back. Winter then relaxed back into the couch and wrapped up into the blanket that was folded on the back of the couch. She wrapped herself up snuggling into the back of the couch, hoping for another nap. Just as she closed her eyes once more, Aaron shrieked in horror. Winter leaped up from the couch, shaking off the blankets as she ran towards the bathroom. She tried to force the door open pushing her right hip against it to help the process.

"Aaron? Are you okay? What's going on?" Winter's voice became higher and filled with worry.

"Aaron, let me in!" Winter kept pushing her body to the door and twisting the knob. Aaron slowly opened the door as Winter collapsed to the floor.

"Oof," Winter swiftly got up off of the floor. Winter's nose tingled as a strange smell invaded her nostrils.

"Are you okay?" Aaron's eyes filled up with salty tears but not one fell to his cheek.

"No, I'm not okay," Aaron yanked the towel from his head and his beautiful perfectly styled hair that they both were so accustomed to, now had a big bald burnt spot at the front center of his head.

Winter immediately covered her face, trying not to laugh at the situation. Dumbfounded and slightly amused, Winter let out a quick giggle under her hand.

"This is not funny, Winter!" Aaron looked into the mirror, inspecting his only bald spot. Winter tried to calm herself before asking, "Ummm… Ah… What… What happened?"

Winter covered her mouth once again, trying even harder now not to laugh at her friend.

"My hairdryer is super old; I've ordered a new one from the salons catalog but I haven't received it yet. I guess I placed my hair too close to the heat for too long and it caught fire," Aaron placed the towel back on his head and shooed Winter out of the bath room. "I have to fix this."

Winter made her way out of the bathroom, still stunned with what had just happened.

"I'm glad you're alive though," Winter joked as she entered the hallway.

Aaron closed the door and spoke through it, "Barely!"

Winter laughed once again. She couldn't remember the last time she laughed this hard and felt this good. She was just glad to be with her friend. This was where she felt most at home, even though her puppy wasn't here. This was her happy place. Winter's Utopia.

Chapter 13
New Beginnings

"Yeah, I want to change my return date."

Winter sat at the tiny kitchen table as she waited for the operator on the phone to help her out. Aaron pointed to the clock on the microwave as she continued on the phone.

"Yes, that's correct."

Winter pressed her face to the phone and lifted her shoulder to hold the phone hands free. She grabbed a pen and paper and wrote down the new time her flight back would be.

"July 24th? Great, thank you."

Aaron clapped his hands softly in excitement as she hung up the phone.

"We got to go, Ashley the tattooist is waiting for us."

Winter quickly shoved the cell phone into her hoodie front pocket and slid on her flip flops she brought with her. They both ran holding hands up the street like a couple of lunatics escaping from the asylum.

"Almost there!"

Both quickly become short of breath started to slow down to a fast pace walk instead of a run.

“So, is she good?” Winter asked as they both now slowed to a normal pace walk.

“She’s great… Just remember when we get the words tattooed just make sure to double check the spelling.”

Winter’s eyes glared over at Aaron, “Why you say that?” Winter let go of Aaron’s hand and continued walking towards the tiny tattoo shop connected to the house down a little further.

“Long story short, my friend, Gloria, got a tattoo from her about three months ago and she asked for beautiful and broken with hearts and butterflies… She got beautiful and broken…but the hearts and butterflies were very nicely done, you almost didn’t notice the word was spelt wrong.”

Winter started to panic as they arrived at the shop door. This wasn’t Winter’s first tattoo but it was the first one she had gotten from a cheap stay at home tattoo artist with dyslexia. They rang the doorbell next to the shop’s door and waited for Ashley to let them inside.

“Hey, you must be Aaron, and you must be Winter,” Ashely smiled. “Come in, come in!”

She took a step back and kept the door open for them as they entered. Ashley was a red headed girl with freckles and beautiful green eyes. She had tattoos all over her arms but nowhere else. Her face was covered in piercings but they didn’t look out of place on her face. Every one of them suited her.

“So, who’s going first?”

Aaron pushed Winter forward, “Winter is!”

Winter clenched her teeth and put a fake smile across her face.

"Yes, I am," Winter muttered as she started to walk to the chair at a leisurely pace. Ashely grabbed a pair of black gloves from a box on the shelf next to her and opened up the needles. Winter stood there watching.

"You said you are getting this on your left calve over the phone, right?"

Winter nodded. Ashley, like a whirlwind, pulled a lever on the side of the chair, which turned it into a little bed.

"Here, lay on your stomach."

Winter looked over at Aaron with discourage in her face. Aaron smirked and did an evil little wave. Winter bit her tongue and lay down onto her stomach and folded her arms, placing her head on top.

"So here are the traces I did from the pictures you sent me through email. Just have a quick look before we get started."

Winter and Aaron double checked the spelling and triple checked just to make sure.

"All good?" Ashley asked as she extended her arm out to take the trace back. Aaron nodded and Winter gave a thumbs up as she laid there slightly shaking.

"Okay, here we go."

Ashley dipped the needle into the ink and placed her hand on Winter's leg. The needle penetrated making Winter jump.

"Ooooo… Hahaha… Oooooo"

Winter's muscles made her bounce.

"Try to stay still." Aaron couldn't keep in his laughter as Winter's laughed in pain, biting her lip, trying not to cry or make loud yelps.

"Yeah, the calve is one of the worse places to get a tattoo."

Ashley added as she kept going.

"Couldn't tell me before hand?"

Winter unintentionally snarked as a wave of she pain traveled up her leg. Ashley stopped and dipped her needle back into the black ink.

"What would be the fun in that?" she replied with a serious face. Winter lifted her head.

Aaron shifted his chair over closer to winter and held her hand, "You got this, sweetie."

About 40 minutes later, Ashley put the tattoo gun down, "There, what do you think?"

Winter stood up and looked into the mirror, "I love it."

It was a perfect friendship tattoo. It had a moon and stars with a swirl design with the words "You see all my light and love all my dark." It was a random quote that both Aaron and Winter loved. They later realized it was from a song by Alanis Morissette called "Everything." It totally suited them and instantly fell in love with it. Ashley wrapped Winter's leg in plastic and handed her a bottle of tattoo cream.

"Don't scratch it until its fully healed. It will get itchy, so just rub this stuff on it so it stays moist and less irritated, okay?"

Winter sat down on the chair Aaron was before her and read the back of the bottle as she waited for Aaron to get his tattoo. Another 40 minutes went by and at last, both of them had new matching tattoos. They took a bunch of pictures and posted them online. They were both so happy with their tattoos.

"So, no matter where we are now, a little piece of each other will be there."

Aaron turned red as he said the cheesiest line he had ever recited. Winter grabbed her friend and gave him a long hug and a kiss on the cheek.

"I love you, man."

"I love you, too, Winter."

They both left the building and started to walk towards home.

"Hey, do you want to grab some grub at the Brittany inns?"

Winter jumped up and down in excited, "Yes, please."

They both rushed the rest of the way home and hopped back into the little blue bug. The roads were clear as they made their way through the small town and to the hotel with the restaurant they always use to go to. It wasn't a fancy hotel or anything but the poutine and buns there was amazing.

"After you, my 'lady," Aaron opened the door for Winter as he pretended to take off an old top hat. Winter curtsied in her imagery dress just before skipping through the hotel doors. The couple behind them gave them hard looks as they walked by.

They always acted silly when they were together. What other people thought of them never bothered them when they were together. They both were better people when they were together. Even though they only met in high school, they acted like they known each other forever.

They both walked inside the restaurant and surveyed the dining hall for the best table. They both sat directly in the middle of the restaurant at a little round table. The table was decorated with a white table cloth and a tiny crystal looking candle. The silverware was wrapped in a black cloth napkin beside an upside-down glass. As they reminisced about old times, a woman wearing a white dress shirt and black dress pants passed them both menus, "Here are your menus, your server, Starla, will be right with you in a moment." The lady walked away and went into the kitchen. Winter leaned in closer to Aaron over the table.

"Starla, as in my ex-best friend, Starla, from school?"

Aaron nodded, "Oops, did I forget to mention that?" Winter sat back into her seat and quickly fixed her hair, looking into her phone's camera.

"You look great, Winter, I did *do* your hair, so..." Aaron giggled at his comment as Winter placed her phone face down onto the table.

"Yeah, I was just checking."

Now Starla and Winter use to be the best of friends. They met in grade three when Starla moved to their little town on the island. Everyone was scared of Starla because she was the tallest one in their grade but one day, they had to do a research project about their favorite animals and had to work in groups. They were placed together and they were forced to hangout. But at that time, it was the best thing that had happened to Winter. She made a new best friend and best friends they were. Both, Starla and Winter, spent every day they could together school, birthdays, summer holidays off school, random coffee trips, sleep overs right up until the end of ninth grade when Winter moved away with her family off the island. Starla and Winter cried when saying their goodbyes, and when Winter was at her new house they talked on the phone almost every day at first, but it slowly turned into every few weeks, months, then it was grade 12 and Winter wanted to graduate with her friends back on the island. She moved back to live with her aunt and uncle while she finished her schooling there. When she went back, she realized just how different they have become and realized the reason why they slowly drifted apart. Starla became more into herself over the years and more serious then she had ever been. She gave off an “I’m better then you” vibe and Winter didn’t enjoy that at all. Winter would try her best to include herself into Starla’s life but quickly realized Starla wasn’t who she used to be. And maybe she wasn’t either. Even though Starla wasn’t excited to see Winter back, everyone else who known her was. Everyone wanted to talk with her and Winter enjoyed seeing everyone again. She was amazed on how much everyone changed in the last few years. They were all young adults now, not just little kids acting dumb. Starla became jealous and envious of Winter and pushed her right out of her life. She pretended to be nice to her to her face but spoke about her behind her back. Winter decided to not fight a relationship with her anymore and gave up. Starla did everything in her power to ignore her and it worked. It hurt Winter at first since she was really hoping things were going to be the same as it was but she was delusional thinking it would be. But, on the plus side, Winter became friends with a beautiful girl named Laura. Laura and Winter had a lot in common and became instant friends. Winter also met Aaron in her computer class after the fall out with Starla. Long story short, Aaron was spitting spit balls at a friend that just so happened to be sitting next to Winter. He missed and hit Winter right in the neck with the biggest, grossest spit ball she ever seen. The saliva ran down her neck and onto her chest before she flung it off and across the room. Aaron apologized and after some prying and nagging, Winter gave Aaron her M.S.N. add. Remember M.S.N. massager? Ahh the good ole days. Anyways and they were best friends since that day. Blah, blah, blah, back to the story.

Starla came out of the kitchen with a jug of water and ice. She strutted her way over to the table.

"Winter? Is that you?"

Winter nodded, "Yeah…it's me."

Starla set the jug of water down on the table and gave Winter a hug.

"So nice to see you, it's been awhile."

Winter slowly nodded her head, "Yup. High school."

Starla Lifted the jug back up and turned the glasses up right and poured, "How long you on the island for?" Aaron crossed his arms and smirked a villainous smirk as he watched the two of them converse.

"Ahh a few months."

Starla stood there, holding the half empty jug of water in one hand and the other hand rested on her hip, "We should totally hang out while you're here. Is your number the same?" Winter nodded once again as she took quick glances at Aaron and back up at Starla.

"Yeah, never changed."

Starla placed the jug on water on the hostess counter to the side of the restaurant and pulled out a pen and note pad from her apron pocket.

"Well, I'll give you a call and we will have to hang."

Winter nodded, "That would be nice."

Just to let you know, Winter haven't seen her since that day. And haven't heard from her since.

Aaron and winter enjoyed their awkward but delicious dinner at the Brittany inns. A few more days went by and in those days, the two friends shared many more laughs together. Winter and Aaron lit another bowl as they finished watching the titanic.

"That bitch could have just shifted over and let Jack on the door with her," Aaron blew his nose in the tissue next to him before taking another toke.

"No, he couldn't, Aaron, I thought that, too, until I watched it again. He tried but the door went under water a little so he stayed off to make sure she would survive."

Aaron sniffed as he passed the bowl over to Winter.

"Oh, how romantic."

Aaron sighed.

"I want to find a man like Jack."

He stood up on the couch and hopped to the coffee table, almost knocking over the drinks they had placed there. Winter shifted back into the couch as Aaron went on his spiel, "I want a man who will sweep me off my feet and love me like Jack loved Rose. He literally gave his life for hers. He didn't even second guess it."

Aaron stretched both his arm out to the side. He looked like Rose when her and Jack went to the front of the boat.

"I wanna fly, Winter."

Aaron closed his eyes and swayed his body as he stood on the table.

"Aaron, I think you smoke too much."

Winter laughed but Aaron quickly cut it off, "Or did I smoke just enough?"

As Aaron spoke, a commercial popped up on the T.V.

"Join today for free. And meet the love of your life tomorrow."

Winter took another draw as Aaron hopped off the table and spun around, "Winter, Lets join a dating site right now!"

Aaron ran into his room and grabbed his laptop from his desk.

"Are you kidding me? You know I tried that before and it didn't go well."

Winter set the pipe and pulled her knees up to her chest.

"Oh, come on, babe, for me?" Aaron got down on his knees and started to beg. "Please, please, please, please." Aaron turned off the pleading and on the puppy dog eyes. He slowly batted his eyes at her until she gave in.

"Fine."

They both hovered over the computer setting up their profiles.

"What picture should I use? The one from hair dressing competition or the one from last week's stoner bonfire?"

Winter laughed and looked at the pictures he was suggesting, "Ooo, the bonfire one. The light from the fire adds a great glow to your face."

Aaron agreed and uploaded his pic onto his profile, "Submit and…done. My profile is live!"

Aaron clapped and pushed the computer over to Winter, "Your turn."

Winter stared at the computer unsure of what to write on her profile. After what felt like hours Winter wrote the perfect profile but had no picture.

"Now a pic."

Winter looked over at Aaron with confusion.

"I don't have any on your computer." Aaron reached behind him and grabbed the digital camera that was sitting on the shelf.

"Smile!"

Winter quickly smiled, "Hey, I wasn't ready."

Aaron wrapped his arm around Winter and showed her the picture he had just taken.

"Beautiful, babe."

Winter sighed and let Aaron do his thing. He put it on his computer and uploaded it to her profile.

"Okay, here we go!"

Aaron and Winter both placed their hands on the keyboard

"One… Two…"

On three, the both pushed enter.

"Now what?" Winter asked.

"Now, we wait."

Aaron and Winter sat in front of the computer and within minutes both of them got messages.

"I got one!" Aaron licked his lips and rubbed his hands together before opening the flashing red envelope on his screen. "Hi, I'm Phil. I'm 23 years old from… Blah, blah, blah… Likes cuddling, movies. Blah, blah, blah, ugh…this guy is boring and he isn't even that good looking."

Aaron closed the computer and pushed it over to Winter.

"Don't worry, Aaron, we literally just joined. There will be lots of other guys interested in you."

Aaron nodded in agreement, "You're right."

Aaron got up from the chair and walked out to the kitchen to grab a glass of water. Winter opened the laptop and logged back into her account. As she opened her mail an astound look over took her, "15 messages already?"

Aaron ran back into the room, "Let me see, let me see!"

Aaron scooched Winter as he sat next to her on the bed. Winter's face turned from surprised to appalled in a matter of seconds, "Ewww, are you kidding me. Here look at this one." Winter turned the screen to Aaron as he moved in closer. He immediately began to laugh, "Oh my land, winter, this guy is a real catch." Aaron laughed once again as Winter's face turned red with embarrassment, "Let me read this out loud to make sure I'm seeing this right."

Winter covered her face up with the nearby blanket, laying at the foot of the bed as Aaron read.

"Hey you look hot in your profile pic, was wondering if you would like to go for coffee with me. And on the way there, you could maybe suck my large cock."

Aaron let out a huge hardy laugh as Winter sunk further into the bed.

"This isn't the romance I was looking for but I mean he does seem adventurous," Aaron elbowed Winter lightly as she chuckled.

"Ugh, I'm deleting this right now!" Winter angrily tried to find the delete account button.

"No, winter, don't, that was just one guy…"

"Have you read the other messages?"

Aaron shook his head, "Well, here's another, *I want you to sit on my dick and never get off.*"

"And the other 13 are basically the same."

Winter clicked a few things and eventually found the magic delete button. With no hesitation, she clicks it.

"Sorry this option is currently unavailable to you. You need to have your account activated for 24 hours before deactivating. Sorry for the inconvenience." Winter slammed the computer shut and laid back in the bed.

"Winter, we will get rid of it tomorrow night. No worries, okay?" Aaron laid next to her and kissed her forehead.

"Why are most guys pigs?" Winter asked in frustration.

"Because, babe, we just are," Aaron held Winter in his arms while he softly played with her hair comforting her until they both fell asleep. Winter woke up bright and early the next morning. She got up and walked out to the living room. She sat on the bench next to the window and watched the sun as it rose. A pretty, little, blue bird landed on the windowsill as Winter admired the view. Winter pressed her hand up against the glass softly wiggling her fingers at the bird. The bird didn't fly away, it just tilted his head and started to peck its tiny beck at Winter's fingers. Winter snickered at the silly, little bird as it tried to eat her fingers. After a few moments of unsuccessfully eating her fingers, the bird flew off.

Winter spent the whole day relaxing around the house with Aaron until the moment came she had been waiting for. An alarm went off on Winter's phone.

"It's time!"

Winter sped down the hall and snatched the computer out of Aaron's hands.

"Hey, I was watching a video of some guy trying to swallow cinnamon. He's like choking, it's great."

Winter shook her head, “No time for that, its account deleting time.”

Winter swiftly pulled up her account and clicked through until she found the button she had been craving to push for the last 23.5 hours. Just when she was going to push deactivate, a red envelope popped up onto the screen. Winter sighed, “Guess, I’ll just check this last one before I delete it forever.”

She clicked open the message and started to read it quietly to herself.

“Hey, I read your profile and I noticed we have a few things in common and we seem to be looking for the same things in life. Your profile picture is very pretty as well. Maybe we could chat a bit and get to know each other. Read my profile and if you’re interested message me back. Have a good day. I hope to hear from you soon.”

Winter’s eyes glistened as she began to read the random guys profile. His picture was him in fire suspenders with a red shirt on that Winter found comical. Poker? I hardly know her. She shook her head and giggled as she admired his white beautiful smile. “Wow…” Winter said aloud as she continued to snoop around his profile. Aaron became instantly curious as became glued to the screen.

“What? Is it not working?”

Winter leaned back in a daze and let out an admiration sigh.

“He’s gorgeous.”

Aaron yanked the computer away.

“He does look like your type.”

He gave Winter back the computer, "So, what is the next step?" Aaron crossed his legs and rested his arms on his knees. Winter sat back up and thought for a moment.

"I'm going to give him my number and delete the account. If he texts or calls then I guess we will see," Winter responded.

"I also ready your profile, I, too, find you attractive and would like to get to know you. I'm deleting my account, but here's my number," she sent the message and deactivated the account.

"What if he doesn't write you?" Aaron wondered.

Winter replied with confidence in her voice, "If he doesn't, he doesn't."

Before she could finish her sentence, her cell vibrated on the bed. Both Winter and Aaron grabbed for it at the same time but Winter got it first.

"Hey its LifeSizedTeddybear, you gave me your number."

Winter bit her lip as her private parts tingled.

"This is going to be fun!"

Winter texted him back right away. They talked all night, and all day and even video chatted a few times. Ninety percent of their conversations were dirty but there was some normal stuff as well.

"You guys have been chatting all day, put the phone away," Aaron urged. Winter put the phone down; as she did, an idea dinged in her head.

"I finally have control."

Winter stood up off the bed and started to pace back and forth the room. Aaron squinted in confusion.

"What do you mean?"

Winter explained, "All my life I've been pushed, walked over and used for other people's pleasure, now I can make my own decision and I can have sex with this guy and never seen him again. Take my life back. Regain control."

Winter continued to pace the room. Aaron leaned back in the chair and rested his feet on the desk.

"Yaaas, bitch, if that's going to help you deal with all your shit, do it!"

Winter looked down at Aaron as she started packing up her things.

"I think it's time for me to go back home."

Aaron widened his eyes and placed his feet firmly on the ground.

"Whoa, whoa, whoa… Right now?"

Winter balled up here clothing that lay around the room and stuffed it into the bag.

"I really need to do this for me. A.S.A.P."

Aaron stood up and gave Winter one of his famous hugs.

"Go, be in control. Get laid, my friend!"

Winter laughed as she continued to pack up her things. Aaron called the company Winter was flying with and changed her ticket once again.

"Okay, hun, you're booked for later tonight. Let me give you a ride to the airport, you crazy bitch."

It didn't take long Winter arrived at the airport.

"I guess this is good bye for another while, huh?" Aaron started to tear up as his friend grabbed her bag from his car.

"It's see you later."

Winter and Aaron hugged in the middle of the Terminal road. Both crying as they embraced.

"Get you shit together, girl! Take back control of your life."

Winter wiped away her tears and then Aaron's.

"I will, thank you."

Aaron stood there in the road until Winter disappeared into the crowd entering the airport.

Winter checked in a found a quiet spot in the airport so she could FaceTime Lifesizedteddybear.

"Hey, sexy, what you doing'?"

Winter smiled as soon as she seen his face on the screen.

"I'm actually on my way back there from my trip."

He smiled back as she told him the news.

"That's awesome, so we will get to meet soon then?"

Winter nodded.

"Can I pick you up from the airport?" he asked with caution in his voice.

"Yes, you sure can."

He bit his lip and moved closer to the camera.

"When I see you, I'm just going to grab your ass and make out with you right there in the airport."

Winter looked over her shoulder, making sure no one was listening to their conversation.

"Do it. Then we can fuck in the back of your truck."

Winter played with her hair as they flirted.

"I gotta go, babe, I'll see you around 11 a.m. at the airport, okay?"

"Sounds good, babe."

Click.

Winter hung up the phone as she did final boarding call for her flight broadcasted on the speakers. Winter ran, dragging her bag behind her. She darted across the hall, swerving her way around the people in the halls. She just made it in time to her gate before they closed the door for boarding. “Phew,” Winter got onto the plane and rested. She was going to miss her friends and family here on the island but she was motivated to get back and start her new beginning.

Chapter 14
Unexpected

Avery jumped up and down as he told Craig the news.

"I'm going to pick her up in like two hours. I'm so nervous."

Craig tried to calm Avery down as he started to have a small panic attack, "Dude, it's going to be good, just be yourself and remember not to rush things. Whatever happens, happens. God has it written already."

Avery nodded as he continued to panic, "What do I wear? What do I say?"

Avery couldn't stand still. His body was to full of adrenalin.

"You know when I had that girl over here a few weeks ago, I wasn't nervous at all. I don't get it."

Avery bounced his leg as he tried to sit.

"You know why you weren't nervous, it's because you weren't expecting it to work anyways, this time, you want a real relationship."

Avery's whole body shook as he bounced in his chair.

"I got to go get ready, bro, Take her easy."

"Talk to you later, bro."

Avery threw the phone onto his bed as he stood up and examined his closet. He grabbed a blue and white plaid shirt off one of the hangers and some beige, cargo shorts. He pulled on the clothing and looked into the mirror and fixed his collar. He took a deep breath and grabbed his truck keys to make his way to the airport. He wanted to make sure he was there on time and not one minute late.

While Avery was driving to the airport, Winter was trying to fix her hair and makeup before landing. She fell asleep on the plane and woke up to rooster hair and raccoon eyes. She grabbed her hairbrush out from her bag and brushed the knots until her hair was silky smooth. She then grabbed her lip gloss that smelt like cotton candy and layered it on. She took out her phone and opened the camera app. Making sure she looked presentable to meet Mr. Teddybear. Avery arrived at the airport and searched for a parking spot. Everything seemed to be full. Avery sees a small sign in the corner of his eye "Cargo loading and drop off zone." Avery shrugged his shoulders and turned into the lane. He parked his truck in the pick-up zone and headed inside. He looked around the airport, making sure he didn't mistakenly come too late. He played around his collar and the buttons on his shirt until he seen her. The woman in the photo online. The girl with the wavy brown hair and the juicy lips. The girl with the blue-ish, green eyes that captivated him as soon as he seen her. The hairs on his neck started to stand as he swiftly made his way over to her while her back was turned. Winter was discretely looking around the airport for the random man that was giving her a ride home. In more ways than one. Straight away, this amazing plan to gain control made her feel vulnerable.

This was a bad idea, she thought to herself. All of a sudden, a big manly hand grasped her ass and a strong arm wrapped around her back and dipped her down as soft lips and a warm tongue passionately kissed her lips. Winter dropped her bag. When the kiss was finished, Avery stood her back up and introduced himself the proper way.

"I'm Avery. Very nice to meet you, Winter."

Winter's face turned beat red as he bent over and grabbed her bag.

"Is this it?" Avery asked. Winter still dazed nodded he grabbed her hand and they both walked hand in hand to the truck. Avery threw her bag into the pan of the truck and opened the door open for her. He lifted her into the truck and kissed her once more before closing the door. His cock was rock hard and she was throbbing just thinking about it. As he tried to hide his boner, a worker from the airport came outside and investigated the truck. "Were you here to pick up cargo, sir?" the lady walked around the truck sizing it up. Avery responded, "Yes, precious cargo." He winked at Winter as he made his way to the driver's seat the lady walked back inside the building. Winter was overly flatter with his charming ways but was very nervous. She had never done anything like this before, she wasn't really sure she wanted to have sex with him right now. Yes, at some point, maybe, but after being hurt so many times, she realized it something that shouldn't be rushed. Avery felt the tension as he drove.

"Hey, we don't have to do anything right now, we can just hang out and see where things go from here, okay?"

Winter's tension faded with his kind words, "Sounds great."

Avery took one hand off the steering wheel and placed it palm up in the middle of the two of them. Winter looked down at his hand and softly placed hers into his. He lifted her hand to his face and gently kissed it. Winter blushed once more. This was definitely unexpected.

Months went by and Avery and Winter became closer each day. It was safe to say they were starting to fall in love. When Avery wasn't in fire meetings or busy working, he spent every minute with Winter. He had never felt this way about anyone before. He was over the moon. He was giddy.

Winter felt the same, she wanted to be ready to give herself to him but she was still nervous about getting hurt. She had trusted others before and it never worked out in the end. Winter tried to hide her brokenness but sometimes, it couldn't be hidden. Her heart craved love but ever since Richard, she distanced herself from the world. Her heart was on guard 24/7. She didn't know what to do anymore.

Avery had finished work and wanted to visit Winter. He missed her touch, her smell her… Everything when they were apart.

He had never been this patient with all the other girls he had been with. Even though he wasn't keeping score anymore, he knew there was something special about this girl, number 37.

Avery knocked on the door and headed inside. He took his shoes off and made his way over the stairs to Winter's room. Winter greeted him at her bedroom door, "Hey, hun. How was work?"

Avery kissed her forehead, "Was okay, missed you though."

Winter smiled a half smile and sat down on the bed.

Avery sat next to her, "What's wrong?"

Winter shifted back onto the bed and rested her back against the wall, "I care about you a lot, like I never have felt this way about anyone before. I'm actually a little scared because my plan was to just have sex and leave but when we kissed, it's like my soul ached and felt complete."

Avery smiled and shifted back onto the bed next to her and continued listening. She rested her head on his shoulder and hugged into him as she spoke.

"I've just been through a lot…"

Winter told him everything. About Mark, Justin, Richard, the whole story. Avery sat there and never budged. He really listened to what she was saying and how she was feeling. He hurt for her and felt her pain, which he had never done before. This girl made him feel and do things he had never imagined doing or feeling. Winter closed her eyes and leaned her head back to the wall.

"If you don't want to be with me, I'll understand, I'm really fucked up. I'm at an all-time low in my life and I don't even know if I'm ready for this."

Avery hugged into her, "I'm not going anywhere, everyone has demons they can't shake off on their own. Sometimes you need extra help getting rid of them." Avery laid his hand softly over hers and gave it a gently squeeze.

"The look in your eyes…. I can tell you love me. I'm not like the other guys, okay? Maybe I use to be, but I'm not like that anymore. I want you and only you. I'm willing to do anything and everything to make you happy. I already know I want to spend the rest of my life with you and I'm willing to wait until you realize that, too."

Tears fell from Winter's face. Avery lightly grabbed her chin with his thumb and his pointer finger and pulled her chin upward and kissed her lips. He gently wiped her tears away before going back in for another kiss. In that moment, winter knew he was different than the rest. She felt safe, warm, and happy. Her body went weak and for the first time in ages, she let her heart truly feel. She let go and trusted Avery with her everything. Avery would ask before he did anything.

"Can I… Is this okay?" Winter nodded as Avery slowly took her shirt off. He kissed her shoulder before asking to take her bra off. Winter smiled and nodded once more as he undid her bra. She leaned her head back in pleasure as he gently sucked on her neck. He slid his hand down her chest and stopped above the belt line.

"We don't have to do anymore if you aren't okay with it."

Winter smiled and moved his hand down as to say it's okay. Avery slowly pulled her pants down her legs and over her feet. He then kissed her from her feet up to her lips. Winter wrapped her arms around his neck as he leaned down to pleasure her clit. His moved his finer gently over her clit, going in a slow circular motion. He kept kissing her as he did. Winter's back arched as he played with her. Winter had never felt so much attention and pleasure in her whole life. Avery leaned back and asked if she wanted him inside. Winter nodded over and over again until Avery took his cock and tease her opening with the tip. He kept teasing her as he kissed her lips. The spark between them was electric. Their eyes met and their souls connected as Winter raised her hips to his. Winter's eyes closed with pleasure as

Avery's cock slid inside her tight wet pussy. Winter moaned in pain and pleasure as he entered her.

"Do you want me to stop? Are you okay?" Avery asked concerned Winter tapped his back.

"Don't stop!"

Avery smirked and continued. Winter kept moaning as Avery started to go faster and harder, making sure every inch was deep inside her. Avery began to moan as well, both of them in sync, came. Winter had never had an organism before. Not with anyone else anyways. They both laid on their backs. Their breaths were heavy and their cravings were satisfied. They both laid there with smiled on their faces. Finally, they had found each other.

A few years later, they got married on March the 7th and had two beautiful children. Even though they lost their first one at ten weeks, they stayed strong and kept trying. Life was almost perfect for Winter and Avery. Yes, they had their fights and arguments but love always won, no matter what they were going through.

Yes, Avery did lose his business, his house, his car, and most of his memories, he gained true love and became a better person. Like the saying I heard a little while ago, you may have heard it, too.

Everything happens for a reason.

Sometimes, we don't understand what the reason is but, in the end, it's usually for the better. Each step, each struggle, Avery went through made him the person he is today and same goes for Winter. Sometimes, you have to walk through shit before you get to smell the roses. And for Avery and Winter, the roses were blooming.

The End.

P.S. Did you noticed they got married on 3-7? March the 7th… And she was the 37th girl he had been with… Ha… What a coincidence huh? Must be something about 37.